TOUGH GUY

JAMIE K SCHMIDT

Tough Guy is a standalone story inspired by Vi Keeland and Penelope Ward's *Cocky Bastard*. It's published as part of the Cocky Hero Club world, a series of original works, written by various authors, and inspired by Keeland and Ward's *New York Times* bestselling series.

Tough Guy is a work of fiction. Names, places, and incidents either are products of the author's imagination or are used fictitiously.

This book is a work of fiction. All names, characters, locations, and incidents are products of the authors' imaginations. Any resemblance to actual persons or things, living or dead, locales, or events is entirely coincidental.

Editor: Jane Haertel, Crazy Diamond Editorial

Photo Credit: DesignRans

Formatted by: Megan Ryder

FREE BOOK

Thank you for buying this book! I hope you enjoy it and would consider leaving me a review.

If you'd like to keep up to date on my new releases and other fun things, please subscribe to my newsletter and get a ***FREE BOOK***.

Be a VIP Reader and have a chance to win frequent prizes, free books, and up to date information.

Your Free Book:

Click Here: https://dl.bookfunnel.com/w9gnkxp12u

My sister lives to ruin my life.

That isn't fair. It's not her fault our dance instructor called me fat and awkward, and our parents funded Lisa's training instead of mine because I had a better head for business.

So when Lisa went off the rails after her injury, it naturally came to me to track her down. The trail starts at the Spearmint Rhino —an upscale gentlemen's club five minutes off the Las Vegas strip, where a group of hot Aussie soccer players are having a bachelor party. *Hello, Chance Bateman!* My sister still wears his jersey as a nightgown. However, Lisa's trail goes cold at Dalton's, which is owned by a world-famous bouncer, Miles Carvello—six feet four inches of muscle, tattoos, and swagger. Combined with his intense green-eyed gaze, Miles makes my insides sizzle. I'm just not sure if Miles Carvello is the reason she's hiding out or not. Danger seems to surround him.

How does a former Broadway hoofer wind up in Vegas as a stripper? I don't know, and no one will talk to me because I'm an outsider. Miles thinks I'm too much of a prude to do what needs to be done.

I need to find my sister. She's in trouble. I can feel it. I keep running into the bachelor party as well as Miles around town while I'm out searching for her. And while all of them are a good time, they're not getting me any closer to finding Lisa. And I've got a terrible feeling that her time is running out.

———

I don't remember Jackie Mitchell's sister. Just another stripper with baggage in a long line of them. But Jackie? Damn, she's the real deal. I don't want to get distracted. I need to shoot this club into the stratosphere. I owe it to my uncle's memory not to let the gangsters win. But she oozes sensuality that reminds me that I should take time to enjoy the finer things in life—like her long, toned legs wrapped around my shoulders.

However, the demons of my past are pushing into my future. If they're going after my employees, as a way to get to me—they picked the wrong guy to mess with. And if they touch Jackie, all bets are off. I'll put them in the ground—and to hell with the consequences.

Tough Guy **takes place a year before the events of** *Cocky Bastard* **and features a few appearances by our favorite Aussie soccer player, Chance Bateman, before he meets the love of his life, Aubrey.**

CHAPTER ONE

Jackie Mitchell

My feet were killing me, and my cheeks hurt from grinning so hard. I aced the audition and got the part. Sure, it was only a minor part in the ensemble in an off-Broadway play, but my dream was finally going to come true. I was going to dance professionally. After four years of college and another four years of being the business manager of my much more talented sister, Lisa, I was free to pursue my dream at long last.

When my phone rang and I saw it was my mother, I almost didn't pick up the phone. She was going to harsh my groove something fierce. I was about to put the phone back into my purse when she called again. She was retired. She could do this all day. I, on the other hand, had to get back to the Zimmerman Agency and make up the time that I'd spent in the audition.

"I can't talk now," I said, navigating the busy Manhattan streets with ease. "I've got to get back to work." There was a bite in the air and it smelled like snow. Shivering, I zipped up my parka and tugged my knitted hat down over my ears.

"You need to drop everything. Get on a plane to Vegas and find your sister." My mother's voice was shrill with hysteria. I rolled my eyes. Just a typical Monday.

"No, I really don't," I said. "Lisa is an adult. She's going through a rough patch, but she'll be fine."

"She should be back here in New York auditioning."

It was on the tip of my tongue to tell her about the part I just got, but I decided I wanted to feel the glow of success for a few more days before my mother pissed all over it. I could hear the sneer in her voice now.

If you're not on Broadway, you might as well be doing community theater.

"I haven't spoken to her in a month and a half." My mother ranted on, oblivious to the argument I was having with her in my head. "She sends a terse text every week. How do I even know it's her?"

"Was Lisa whining or feeling sorry for herself?" That slipped out before I could stop it. It would have been fair game, except in my sister's last starring role—yes, on Broadway—she tore the hell out of her ACL and the doctors didn't think she was ever going to dance professionally again.

Since that had been her identity for her entire life, Lisa was taking it understandably hard. She had aced her physical therapy, but the moment she could walk again without crutches, she was on the plane to Vegas. I guess New York City had too many memories for her.

"She tells me she's fine and not to worry. And then I ask her if she went on any auditions this week and she doesn't answer. I haven't even gotten a text from her in two weeks. Nothing."

"Last I heard she was bartending at a strip"—I coughed to cover my slipup—"er, high-end club on the Strip." Actually, it was a gentlemen's club called the Spearmint Rhino about five miles from the Strip, but who's counting?

My mother would. She'd probably think that if it wasn't on the Las Vegas Strip, Lisa might as well be mixing drinks in her apartment.

"Have you heard from her?"

I squinted and scrolled through my messages. "No, not for over a month."

"You girls don't keep in touch? Aren't you supposed to be booking her for jobs?"

The accusation in her tone stiffened my back. "Her contract is on hiatus with the Zimmerman Agency." It was a long-term hiatus, considering my sister's knee couldn't take the strain of a show at this time. Maybe even never. I pushed down the pity. I knew what it was like to have your dream snatched from you. But no one ever coddled me or even thought twice about my feelings.

I pinched my nose. I thought I had worked through all these feeling in therapy, but apparently not.

"Jaqueline Aida Mitchell, you are your sister's advocate. That's what we're paying you to be."

I wanted to hurl the phone into traffic. "Actually, I get fifteen percent of what she brings in, so if she doesn't get paid neither do I." And my mother knew that. She was trying to "motivate" me in that special way that she had. One that usually wound up with me doing something stupidly competitive to prove I was just as good a daughter as Lisa.

"So why aren't you out there hustling for her?"

"Mom, she can't dance."

There was a horrified silence, and I hoped she'd hung up on me, but my luck was never that good.

"You shut your mouth," she finally said. "You are not a doctor."

"I'm hanging up now," I told her.

"Wait," she screeched.

"Be nice," I warned.

"Your father and I are worried sick." My mother lowered her voice. "He's drinking again."

"Damn it," I said, leaning against the light post as I waited for the orange walk sign to come on. She was really firing all the guilt arrows today.

"It would mean the world to us—to him, if you could track your sister down and make sure she's all right. These texts don't even sound like her. What if she's in trouble? I know in my gut something is wrong. It would ease our minds —your father's mind—if you would go out there and see that she's coping with the hiatus."

I hated that she pulled the Dad card out. Dad, when he was sober, was the parent who always had my back instead of Lisa's. From looking the other way when I broke curfew to lending me a hundred bucks when things were tough, he was the parent I went to when I needed one.

"I have a job." I tried to keep the whine out of my voice. I was caving and I knew it. It made me so mad. *Why do I let her do this to me every time Lisa flakes out?* "I can't just drop everything to look for Lisa. She obviously wants to be alone."

"Or she's been kidnapped or is on drugs or is being taken advantage of."

"Did you call the police?" A wiggle of doubt crept in, despite my best efforts.

"Of course, I did. They laughed at me. They said trying to find one dancer in Las Vegas even when there was a verifiable crime was next to impossible. Without a suspicion of one, they're not even going to look."

"I'm sure there are more pressing matters for them."

"Nothing is more important than your sister."

And that was the story of my life. I was done trying to prove that I was just as important, wasn't I? I wasn't expecting that this time when I pulled off the impossible, my mother would smile at me proudly. I was twenty-six. Why did I still crave her approval? And yet, what if Lisa *was* in trouble and I ignored it? I'd never forgive myself.

I rubbed my hand over my face and let the crowd push me forward across the busy street when the light turned. "You're overreacting. You know that, right?"

"What if I'm not?"

I was going to lose the bit dancing part that I had worked so hard for. I was going to have to put my life on hold because of Lisa. Again. It was the story of my life and I was sick of it. I should tell my mother that I was the better dancer now, and I was going to work my way up to be a Broadway star. But I was afraid of her laughter and her derision. I had survived it once when I was thirteen and she yanked me out of dance class. We could only afford one set of lessons and Lisa was a prodigy who had been getting offers before she was ten.

I was the smart one. Lisa was the talented one.

Blinking back tears, I opened my mouth to tell my mother off. But I couldn't do it. Lisa had sunk down into a dark place after the doctors told her she'd never dance again. Mom didn't know about the pills Lisa took or how I'd held her hand after they pumped her stomach. Guilt nibbled at me.

"Did you hear the nor'easter is going to dump a foot of snow on us this weekend?" a man walking next to me said into his Bluetooth.

I recoiled. Ugh. It was bad enough that the wind was chapping my cheeks raw now. I wasn't looking forward to trudging through ankle-deep slush and dirt for weeks.

"Did you hang up on me?" My mother's shrill voice knocked me out of my thoughts. "When are you leaving for Las Vegas?"

A foot of snow. Or tooling around in the desert in Sin

City. Suddenly, there was a little sugar to go with the bitter coffee my mom was pouring down my throat.

Maybe I was approaching this the wrong way. Lisa was probably fine, but my mother wouldn't leave either one of us alone until she knew for sure. The casting director really liked me. There would be another audition soon and I'd ace that too. I could have a mini vacation and find Lisa. It was a win-win situation.

A little flutter of excitement started in my stomach. I loved Las Vegas. I'd had some good times on spring break there. A few memories made me blush and shake my head. I was lucky I wasn't caught on a *Girls Gone Wild* video. That was how out of control I'd gotten in the clubs down there.

Las Vegas was a hell of a temptation even when you weren't a carefree coed. Lisa could very well be in over her head. Or she could be having the time of her life. There was something about the town that encouraged you to go crazy and do things you would never in your right mind do anywhere else. On my twenty-first birthday, I took a bouncer home and had a hot-and-heavy one-night stand that I still thought about. Vegas was a good time.

I deserved another no-holds-barred week to make it up to myself for giving up the job to dance on stage in order to find my pain-in-the-ass sister. After all, what happens in Vegas stays in Vegas, right?

"Lisa doesn't have a lot of money in her escrow account," I said. "And I can't afford to pay for this out of pocket."

"How much is this going to cost me?" my mother said flatly.

"We don't have to do this, you know."

"Fine. Put it on your credit card and send me an expense report. What Lisa's royalties and residuals won't pay for, I'll cover."

I pumped my fist. I was getting smarter at dealing with

my mother. She had the time and discretionary funds to drop everything and get on a plane. I didn't. I still needed to work to pay my bills and make rent. This adventure was going to cut in on my bottom line. "I'm going to need some spending cash," I pushed.

"I'll wire you two thousand dollars and not a dime more. And I want every cent accounted for."

I blinked. That was twice what I was going to ask for. She was serious if she was dipping into her bank account. Despite having inherited a ton from her parents, my mother was a notorious tight wad.

"Don't you dare blow it in the casinos."

Rolling my eyes, I pictured myself throwing dice on a craps table. I didn't even know how that worked. Did I want a seven? Did I want snake eyes? She should have warned me not to blow it all on spa treatments because that was more my style. So I would have cash, my expenses would be paid, and I'd be out of the snow. I should be overjoyed. Instead, I felt like I had taken a huge step backward in my career and life.

"I'll call you when I land," I said, but there was a part of me already regretting my decision. I needed to stop letting my mother and sister dictate my life. And I would. Just not today.

CHAPTER TWO

Miles Carvello

I dodged a punch, grabbed the asshole's wrist, and twisted his arm behind his back. "Not in my bar, motherfucker," I told him and literally kicked his ass out of Dalton's.

My bouncers were the best money could buy on or off the Las Vegas strip—and we were very much off the Strip, which probably is why these drunken frat boys thought they could get away with this kind of shit in my club.

"You need help, mate?" Chance Bateman said. He and some of his soccer buddies were sitting on barstools with their backs to the bar, itching to get into the fight. Chance and I went way back when I took a bottle in the head for him at an unruly club in Sidney. He was a great guy—bloke, as he said. It was a shame that he only played one game professionally before an injury sidelined his career for good.

"We got this," I said. "You boys keep drinking and watching the girls." That was all I needed. Five half-crocked Aussies "helping" me.

"What's a bachelor party without a biffo?" Chance grinned and slid off his seat.

Hell no. I looked over my shoulder and gave a sharp whistle. Kikki, Betty, and Nalia wound their way through the combatants toward the private lounge, their tassels shaking from all the right places.

"I've got a better idea," I said, tugging Chance back. "Why don't you take the groom and the rest of the blokes over to the VIP lounge? Free champagne beer for as long as the fight out here lasts."

"Good man." Chance clapped me on the shoulder and herded his team into the area where my three best exotic dancers had just entered.

I needed to get this fight over quickly before the Aussies drank me into bankruptcy. Wading into the brawl, I separated the frat boys from the other patrons. When they swung at me, I swung back. They went down regretting their actions, nursing a swollen jaw or trying not to puke from a well-placed gut or kidney punch. Luckily, after a few more of the frat boys were shown the error of their ways and the door, the rest went willingly. Aside from a couple of scratches and a few bruises, my bouncers came out of the fight all right. As they drifted back to their stations, I saw a bunch of patrons leave. Fighting wasn't good for business, but sometimes I didn't get the choice. Most days I felt like Billy the Kid. But instead of gunslingers coming to test their skills against me, I got college kids on vacation throwing hands.

I was proud of my reputation as an ass kicker. The tabloids named me a "celebrity bouncer" when I was working the club scene in Europe in my twenties. I had thought it was ridiculous, but one of the club owners told me that reputation was everything. If he advertised that Miles Carvello was head of security, the troublemakers usually stayed home—or more likely, found another club to act up in.

The stage show tonight had stopped when the frat assholes started chucking bottles at each other. I walked into the dressing room to check on the girls. I used to knock first, but the dancers kept laughing at me. So now, I just walked right in.

"You guys all right?"

"Fuck," Ginny said, hiding the packets of pills behind her back.

I locked eyes with her buyer, one of the frat boys who was back here hooking up with drugs rather than brawling. "Get out."

He must have already been high because I saw the moment he decided to try me. I went up on my toes to pivot out of the way and I planned to smash him in the mouth with an elbow.

"No," Ginny said, stepping in front of the swing.

Cursing, I yanked her back and we crashed into the vanity table in front of the mirror. The kid pulled a knife, eyes wild. "Give me the pills. And your wallet."

Shoving Ginny behind me so she wouldn't get in my way again, I charged the little bastard. He swung his arm back to swipe at me, but I outweighed him by a good hundred pounds. I tackled him into the ground. He hit his head hard on the shag carpet and the knife went flying. Dragging him up by the hair, I marched him to the back door and threw him down the cement steps to the alley. He made a satisfying crash when he hit the garbage bags.

I toggled on the two-way earpiece I wore. "The frat is banned for tonight. No one wearing their letters is allowed in."

"You got it, boss," my head bouncer said. Highway was a former marine and looked like a meaner version of Clint Eastwood in his day.

The back door locked behind me as I returned to the

dressing room. Ginny was sitting on a stool, posing seductively. Yeah, she was in deep shit and she knew it. She was a busty redhead who knew how to work a room. She had regulars, whom I'd assumed kept coming back to Dalton's to watch her work the pole to David Guetta. Now I had to wonder if that was really the draw.

"Where's everyone?" I asked. There should have been four other dancers back here.

"Mingling."

"Did they know you were selling?"

"Miles," Ginny said, standing up. She attempted to put her arms around my neck, but I blocked her, maybe a little harder than I had to, but I was pissed. I had very strict rules.

1. No sex in the VIP room.
2. No selling drugs.
3. Come to work sober.
4. Don't steal.
5. Come to me if there's a problem.

Ginny rubbed her arms and tried giving me a sultry pout. "It's only some Zannies and Kickers."

"Get your shit and get the fuck out."

"You're firing me?" Her voice rose in disbelief.

"Leave the pills."

"You can't do that," she said.

"Leave them or I call the cops."

"You bastard," she snarled. "You're going to keep them for yourself."

I shrugged. "I'll tell you what. If you tell me who your supplier is, I'll let you keep the pills."

"You don't want to do this." Ginny tried one last seduction, looking at me under long thick lashes. "I'll be good. I won't do it again. I promise." She slinked closer to me, pouting her crimson lips again. "I'll do anything for a second chance." Smiling, she sank down to her knees with a practiced ease.

"Who gave you the drugs to sell out of my club?"

Ginny scowled and rocked back on her heels. "Are you kidding me? Who cares? I'll cut you in if you want."

"The name or get the fuck out of my club."

"Go to hell." She stood up. Stormed over to the closet and grabbed her trench coat. Wrapping it around herself, Ginny glared. "You just want to corner the market. You think you're the only game in town? You're nothing. This bar is nothing." She pulled out a drawer full of bells and flimsy things and stuffed the contents into her coat pockets.

"Don't let the door hit you on the ass on the way out," I said.

"You're going to regret this. Biggest mistake of your life."

"It's not even in the top ten." And it wasn't.

She paused in the doorway. "I really liked you. You were a cool boss, until you weren't. Just remember, you brought this on yourself." Tossing her hair, Ginny flounced out with all the drama of a pissed-off stripper. And she hadn't given up her supplier.

Scooping up the several baggies of pills, I walked through the club to my office in the back. I was going to stow the drugs in my safe until the next time Grier showed up. The undercover cop and I had an agreement. I'd give him all the intel I had on any drugs moving around this side of town and he'd keep the investigation into my uncle's death two years ago from gathering dust on a desk.

Uncle Johnny had taken me in when my parents spiraled down into gambling and drugs. He let me sleep in the backroom of his burlesque club when they lost the house. He gave me a job cleaning up the club after school, so I had a place to go. Then the bouncers thought they could use a kid of my size and they trained me. The martial arts lessons paid off and I worked my way through high school minding the door and managing drunks. I should have never left for Europe. Uncle Johnny and his club might still be here if I hadn't been gallivanting all over world, having one big party.

I had just opened the safe when the hairs on the back of my neck stood up. Expecting a fight, I whirled on the balls of my feet.

Chance leaned drunkenly against the door frame. He held out his hands in front of him. "Easy mate. Whatcha got there?"

Pitching the baggies into the safe, I said, "They're not for sale." Locking it, I turned back to Chance, who hadn't moved.

"Not looking to buy drugs, mate. Looking for more girls."

I clapped him on the shoulder. "That I can help you with."

CHAPTER THREE

Jackie Mitchell

Because I was expensing this trip to Lisa's account, I booked a room at the Wynn on the Las Vegas Strip instead of one of the budget hotels closer to the airport. I considered it compensation for having to turn down the part in the show. Although after visiting her apartment in New York and having her roommates tell me that Lisa took all her stuff and moved out three months ago, I was no longer thinking that Lisa was just flaking out for longer than usual.

She'd actually moved to Vegas. Who did that? Vegas was for playing around, doing daring and stupid things, before returning back to the drudgery of your existence. You didn't live here. You risked having the shine buffed out of the town. I'd figured she was just on an extended vacation, but she'd given up her Brooklyn pad to go live in the desert.

Alone in my luxury room, I quickly unpacked and then did a few arabesques and pliés because I wasn't used to having so much room to move. My apartment back in Queens was so tiny that Lisa could touch her fingertips on one wall and her toes on the other. I was slightly shorter, so that was another thing that she did better than me. I wonder what apartments looked like here. Too bad I didn't have Lisa's address. She hadn't shared it with our parents either.

I called her, but it went to voice mail again. "Hey, Lisa. It's me. I'm in Vegas. I need to see you. Please don't make me track you down. I'm at the Wynn in room 1492. Give me a call and we can get drinks or something."

I didn't have any hopes that she would call or text back. She'd gone incommunicado, and I had to admit that even I was starting to buy into my mother's paranoia. When she didn't immediately call me back, I decided I better start my Nancy Drew routine. My first stop was the Spearmint Rhino, a titty bar about five miles off the Strip and Lisa's last known location. I parked my rental car in a nearby garage and walked to the club.

The Spearmint Rhino was glitzy and neoned up enough to be on the Strip, but I'd bet it saved a ton on rent by not being there. The doorman seemed about to give me grief. I wasn't dressed to impress. I wore a Calvin Klein wrap dress and sensible-heeled sandals. But after a quick look around, he must have decided that it was early enough in the night to let me in. In another few hours, I'd be waiting on line for a miracle and paying a hefty cover charge—if I even managed to get past the guy.

"Thank you," I murmured and slipped him a twenty. That seemed to brighten him up a bit. Until I asked about my sister. He just grunted and gestured for me to go inside. I wasn't sure if that was good news or bad news.

The beer, burgers, and boobies happy hour was still in effect. Not interested in any of those, I sat down at the bar and exchanged a tired smile with the female bartender.

"Are you lost?" she asked.

"I'm not, but my sister is."

"There's a lot of that going on around here. Can I get you something?"

I ordered a glass of wine and paid with another twenty. "Keep the change," I said, and slid my sister's headshot across the bar. "Do you know Lisa Mitchell?"

She looked surprised. "Yeah, she worked here about a month ago. I hope nothing's happened to her."

"Me too. She hasn't been in touch for a while and my parents are worried. Do you know why she left?"

The bartender frowned in thought. "I can't say for sure. We didn't have a lot of shifts together and when we did, we were slammed. I know money was an issue with her. That and she was always criticizing the dancers, saying she could do better. It didn't make her very popular around here."

That sounded like Lisa. "Do you think I could talk to the dancers?"

"If you got the money, they've got the time."

I inwardly winced. "Who would you recommend I speak with?"

"If you've got a hundred dollars, you can probably get fifteen minutes in the VIP room at this hour." She leaned over the bar and whispered. "Pay cash if you have it."

"Thanks." Great. Just great.

I caught the eye of one of the dancers who had been doing leg exercises like the ones I had been doing in the hotel room. The only difference was I hadn't been in my bra and panties. Squaring my shoulders, I walked up to her.

"Can I buy fifteen minutes of your time?" I asked.

"First time in a strip club, honey?" she asked.

"Yeah, but I'm not looking for a lap dance. I wanted to ask you some questions."

She looked me up and down. "Most guys like a little jiggle in the wiggle. But you have good muscle tone."

I was ridiculously pleased by that. "I'm a dancer, too," I said.

Glancing around the empty club, she sighed. "I can spare the time. It's a hundred dollars and a two-drink minimum."

I tanked the wine I was drinking. "Does that count?"

"No."

Shrugging, I said, "Okay, let's go." Reaching into my purse, I pulled out a bill and handed it to her. The expense report from this trip was going to be a hoot. I tried to imagine my mother's face when she saw line item: Stripper-VIP dance. Hey, she'd said not to blow it all in the casino. There was nothing in her warning about exotic dancers. Bribes would also be an equally amusing entry on the ledger. I'd have to give it more thought and get creative to save my mother from having an aneurysm.

She tucked it into her bra. "I'm Cookie."

"Jackie," I said, following her into a ten-by-ten foot room.

"Two drinks," she reminded me. "Thirty bucks."

"Jeez." I coughed, but quickly recovered when she glared. "What would you like to drink?" I asked.

Cookie considered it for a minute. "Rum and Diet Coke."

"Get two. With Bacardi."

"Big spender," she said. "Most of the guys go for the well booze."

Placing a hand on my stomach, I grimaced. "Life's too short to drink cheap rum."

"I can get you top shelf," she said hopefully. "It's just a little extra."

"Bacardi is fine."

She came back with two iced-filled glasses. Each was garnished with a cherry. "You're not going to believe who's out there," she said.

"Who?" I asked.

"Chance Bateman. He's an Australian soccer player."

"Yeah?" Smiling, I remembered that Lisa had had a crush on him. There had been a poster of him in her bedroom. "I don't suppose this girl is with him?" I showed her Lisa's headshot.

Cookie squinted at the picture and snorted. "She wishes. No, it's a bachelor party. They were here last night too, but they left early. So we've got to make this quick. I need to be part of that action. They tip large and are real easy on the eyes. Do you want me to take my top off?" she asked, sipping on her drink.

"That won't be necessary. I'm looking for my sister Lisa. She worked as a bartender here about a month and a half ago." I handed her the picture so she could get a better look.

"Oh, that bitch." Cookie sat down and crossed her legs. She took a deep pull from the drink.

Yeah, that was Lisa. I waited for an elaboration, but Cookie just frowned at her glass.

"I hate that they water the drinks down," she said.

"I figured they'd overpour to get the customers to spend more freely."

"Exactly." Cookie pointed a long red nail at me. "But that's not until later when the guys with the deep pockets come in." She looked at the clock on the wall. "Ten minutes, unless you want to pay for extra time."

"Do you know where Lisa is now?"

Cocking her head, Cookie frowned. "I think she went over to Dalton's on Flamingo Road."

"Dalton's?" I searched on my phone. "It's another strip bar." And it didn't look half as upscale as this one. "Why did she go there?"

"Because she bombed her first night on the pole and Nick wouldn't let her back on stage."

I blinked at Cookie in disbelief. "The pole?"

Putting her drink down, Cookie walked over to the stripper pole in the room and did a graceful, lovely circle around it. Coming to a stop, she said, "Your sister was a shitty stripper."

———

Miles Carvello

I watched Chance doing his Magic Mike impersonation up on the stage and couldn't decide if I should hustle him off or take blackmail pictures on my phone. It was the second night of his friend's bachelor party and they were bar hopping all over the place. They'd just cruised in from the Spearmint Rhino crocked out of their minds.

Highway raised his eyebrow at me, and I shook my head. Chance was attracting a crowd that was throwing money and buying drinks. After the fiasco last night with the frat boy fight, I was willing to let Chance entertain the masses while my girls made some real coin on lap dances and private shows.

I saw out of the corner of my eye that a woman was approaching me hesitantly. I was prepared to ward off a horny pass from a customer. I could see how watching Chance could work some women up. But when I turned, I knew right away that this chick was in the wrong place.

She had short blond hair and a killer body that was covered in a bland dress. She moved like a dancer, but was out of her element in the strip club. When she saw me watching her, she stumbled and then blushed. When was the last time I saw someone blush? Definitely not around here. But then Chance's gyrations caught her attention. Her jaw dropped and she stopped dead in her tracks to goggle at him.

That pissed me off for some reason. I wasn't the greatest looking guy in the world, but I wasn't about to get upstaged by a pretty boy Aussie. I got between her and the stage. She had to crane her neck to look up at me.

"Can I help you, Miss?" I asked.

"Is that Chance Bateman?"

"You watch Australian football?" I scoffed in disbelief.

"No, but my sister bought a calendar with him and his teammates on it." She tried to crane her neck around me, but I moved with her. "Let's just say February was a popular month in our house. I thought he was at the Spearmint Rhino tonight?"

"Are you a stalker or a reporter?"

"Neither." She tried to peer around me again.

"Weren't you looking for me?" I growled, blocking her line of sight.

"Oh," she said, visibly shaking herself. "Yes. I was. That is, if you're Miles Carvello?" I saw her look at my tattoos. "Of course you are. The doorman said you might have a moment for me."

I glared up at Highway, who was grinning at me from the door. He knew I liked sassy blondes. "Depends. Who are you and what do you want?"

"My name is Jackie Mitchell. I'm here to find my sister, Lisa."

"Feel free to look around," I said, reluctantly stepping aside.

"I will, but I was wondering if you could tell me if she's taking a shift tonight."

I gawked at her for a moment. "Your sister's a dancer?"

Jackie bit her lip and my eyes riveted on her full mouth before I forced myself to look back into her pretty green eyes. I had to concentrate on what she was saying instead of being distracted by her. On any other night, I'd take her into my office and we'd talk over drinks. If I was lucky, drinks would turn to dinner and other intimate matters and then breakfast. But lately with the fights and Ginny selling drugs out of my club, I was ready to crawl out of my skin. I had a bad feeling there was something going on here and whoever was behind it was just waiting for me to drop my guard before dumping the real shit all over Dalton's.

She handed me a picture and, for the life of me, I couldn't place her sister. I slowly shook my head. "Her face doesn't ring a bell. Do you have a body shot of her?" That was probably the wrong thing to say, because Jackie looked stunned but then she recovered.

"I can access her portfolio from my phone. Do you have Wi-Fi?"

"What kind of exotic dancer has a portfolio?" I asked before I could stop myself.

"One that used to dance on Broadway," Jackie said tartly.

That was familiar. "Broadway. That was her stage name. Yeah, now I remember."

Jackie's shoulders eased in relief. "Is she here?"

"Broadway? No, she quit after a week. She danced a few times and then never showed up to work again."

"When was that?"

I blew out a sigh and stared out at the stage, not seeing the current dancer while I tried to remember the last time Broadway had worked. "I don't know. About a month ago, maybe less."

The nibbling on her lower lip began again and I was again transfixed. What was it about this chick and her mouth?

"Can you give me her home address?"

"I'm going to need some proof that you are who you say you are, and a damn good reason why I should violate your sister's privacy before I do that."

"Can we talk in private?" Jackie put her hand on my arm.

Pure lust flooded me, and I was surprised by the force of it. I've had full lap dances with tits in my face that didn't get me as hard as her full pink lips and the light touch on my skin just had.

"Come with me." Because my dick seemed to be in charge of my brains, I led her into a VIP booth instead of my office.

CHAPTER FOUR

Jackie Mitchell

"Do I have to pay you a hundred bucks and buy a two-drink minimum?" I followed him to a room with a stripper pole and a couch. The space was small and he filled it up. *Try not to make a fool of yourself and drool all over him.* But every hormone I had woke up and screamed, "Hell yeah!" each time his eyes met mine.

"Depends," he drawled, swinging a circle around the pole with more grace than a man of his bulk should have been able to do. "Do you want me to dance?"

The answer should have been no. I was here for my sister. But this was Vegas, right? I was also here to have a good time. And Miles Carvello looked like Good Time was his middle name. After all, I'd missed Chance Bateman gyrating in his boxers. I deserved a little eye candy. I was taking too long to answer and Miles's dark brown eyes got even darker. If he pulled off his shirt, I was a goner. Swallowing hard, I tried to take my eyes off his muscles and the outline of tattoos peeking over his tight white T-shirt. I had a thing for tough guys, what could I say?

Focus, Jackie. Business first. Pleasure hopefully later.

"Do you want to see my ID?" I asked as he took a step closer to me.

He stopped dead in his tracks. "You're not twenty-one?"

"Thanks for that. I meant to convince you I'm legit so you can give me Lisa's information." I fumbled in my purse for my driver's license and business card.

"Lisa who? Oh, right. Broadway."

My head was spinning. Why would Lisa leave a career in New York to dance in a second-rate club for dollar bills stuffed into her underwear? I knew she had medical bills, but she was on a payment plan. "Do exotic dancers make a lot of money?" I sat down on the couch, sinking into it slightly. It was surprisingly comfortable. I wanted to kick off my sandals and relax. The rum and Coke I'd had at the Spearmint Rhino mellowed me out more than I had expected.

"Depends," Miles drawled.

"On what?"

"How good of a salesperson they are." Instead of joining me on the couch, Miles pulled up a chair. Turning it backwards, he straddled the seat and folded his arms on top.

That was not the answer I was expecting. He must have sensed my confusion because he elaborated.

"My best dancer was a Harvard MBA."

"Oh, come on," I scoffed.

"I find the nice, quiet college girls are the wildest." His grin was full of sin and his knowing once-over made me wonder if he had been in the crowd watching me go wild on my twenty-first birthday.

I cleared my throat. "Why was she the best stripper? Was she a classically trained dancer?"

Shaking his head, Miles said, "Because she could do math."

"I hate math."

"Most people do. But if you do four VIP sessions in an hour, how much do you make?"

"Four hundred dollars."

"I take half."

"Half? That's bullshit." I only took fifteen percent of my client's salary. Fifty percent was ridiculous.

He smirked. "My building. My booze. My protection."

I admired his large arms and broad chest. I wouldn't want to get into a fight with him. "Okay, fine. I'll give you that."

"So, you wind up making two hundred dollars an hour. For a six-hour shift, the most you can make is twelve hundred dollars—and that's only if you book back-to-back sessions, which most girls don't."

"What about tips?"

"That's the name of the game. If they're not in the VIP room, they can still make money doing twenty-dollar lap dances."

"Do they do forty-two-hour work weeks?" That would be every day. Seven days straight of dancing was tough.

"If they want. But most of them work four days on and four days off."

It hurt, but I did the math in my head. Maybe that drink hadn't been so watered down after all. "I guess someone who was driven could think she could walk away with twenty-five thousand dollars after a month." Was that why Lisa decided to stop being a bartender? By the end of the year, she could have paid off her medical bills.

"That's a high goal. Like I said, that's only if you're booked solid. No one here has ever been booked solid. The real money comes in tips. I don't take a penny of the dancers' tips. That's 100% free and clear. So when they get the customer into the VIP room, they have to give them an experience that they're not getting on the floor."

"What kind of experience?" I asked warily.

"Not what you're thinking. Out there," I jerked my thumb behind me. "The clients can't touch the girls and they move on after one song unless the guy pays for another lap dance. In here, it's a more intimate one-on-one show."

I took in a sharp breath.

He held up a hand. "I'm not running a whorehouse. I'm legit. But most guys will tip Jacksons to have a beautiful woman give him one hundred percent of her attention for fifteen minutes. Believe it or not most of the guys just want to talk to a naked woman while she's dancing. That's it."

"No funny stuff?" I asked, fascinated despite myself.

He smirked. "Guys don't want a girl to make them laugh."

Rolling my eyes, I said, "I mean what about touchy feelies?" I made groping motions with my hands.

"Legally, you can't do anything lewd. There's a line not to cross."

"What's the line?"

"A little grinding is okay. Maybe a kiss or a nuzzle. The key is to make the guy feel special. Harvard knew that. She could make a grand in the time it took the other dancers to earn a hundred."

"What did she do that made her so popular?"

"Anything the client wanted that she was willing to do."

Crossing my arms in front of me, I said, "I thought you said you weren't running a whorehouse."

He lifted his hand in mock surrender. "I get undercover cops in here all the time and I've never had a solicitation violation. Besides, there are cathouses a quick taxi ride from here where it's all legitimate and you get what you pay for."

"Yeah, you're a perfect angel."

"Not even close."

Damn. I blew out a shaky sigh. I had to stop enjoying talking to him so much. I was on a mission. "I can't see Lisa letting strange men grope her."

"It doesn't have to be groping. It can be sweet talking and pushing drinks. It can be entrancing them with their bodies, teasing as an art form."

"There's got to be guys that take it too far," I said shakily.

"Mav," Miles barked.

I flinched at his tone and the couch sucked me in deeper.

About ten seconds later, the door got kicked open and a giant man stood there glaring into the room with a telescoping baton in his hand. His gaze skated over me and I almost peed in terror. I saw a slight frown cross his brow as he realized it was just me and Miles in the room.

"You need help subduing this one, boss?" he drawled.

"We're good, Mav," Miles said, without turning around to look at him. His dark eyes on mine were amused.

"You sure? Because she looks like she could be trouble."

"Fuck off."

"You called me," Mav grumbled, storming out of the room.

"Close it behind you," Miles said.

The door slammed.

"He was listening in the whole time?" I asked.

"No. Our system responds to keywords. Calling his name or mine triggers an emergency signal that tells security what room and what dancer needs us."

"What happens then?"

His smile turned darker. "I earn my fifty percent."

Well, that explained why Mav came in like a freight train. "I see."

"I take the safety of my staff very seriously. The dancers are in total control in this room. If a customer tries to assault one of my dancers, they get arrested and banned from my establishment—after I bang them against the wall a few times. If you think Broadway met a dark end, it didn't happen in this bar."

"I'm pretty sure she didn't." I told him the story of Lisa's accident. I left out the part about the pills, but played up how worried my parents were. "She shouldn't have been dancing at all."

He smirked. "Vegas turns saints into sinners."

"Don't I know it." I almost choked when he turned interested eyes on me. "But that's not what I meant. Yeah, my mom would shit a brick sideways if she knew her precious ballerina was stripping. But I don't give a shit. Frankly, I'm surprised she unclenched enough to dance to "top forty." I did air quotes on the last two words and said them in Lisa's snottiest tone.

Miles smirked. "She did dance to *All that Jazz*."

I made a face. "That wouldn't be my first choice."

"What would be?"

I pictured it for a moment and was scandalized that the thought of shedding my clothes and dancing was turning me on. "Um. There are a lot of sexy Broadway songs." I needed to focus. This conversation was getting out of hand. "But that's not the point. Lisa could destroy her knee entirely and not be able to walk again. Standing up for an eight-hour shift as a bartender would've been hard enough for her. I'm wondering if the promise of easy money made her get up on the stage."

"It's not easy money. Only the girls who can skate the line of sex and string the mark along with promises and sweet talk are the moneymakers. It's not for everyone and there's a high burnout rate for those who can't separate the fantasy of the job from the reality of it."

I tried not to dwell on the sound of the word *sex* coming out of his mouth. "Was Lisa a moneymaker?"

"Broadway?" He snorted. "No."

I nodded. "Then it's possible she tried stripping as a lark and when she didn't make any money, she moved on to something else."

Miles nodded. "Happens all the time."

That made me feel a little better. "That doesn't leave me any closer to finding her, though. Is there anything you can do to help?"

"Normally, I don't do this," he said. "But let me make a few inquiries and if your story checks out, I'll give you the address she gave me on her employment application."

"Thanks." I sagged back into the couch in relief. "Do you mind if I ask some of the dancers if they know where she is?"

"As long as you pay for their time."

"Can I have seltzer instead of booze for the drink minimum?" I asked. "I'm a little buzzed from the last rum and Coke I had at the Spearmint Rhino."

Miles stretched up from the chair. My eyes riveted on the strip of abs that flashed when he stood up. Wow. I swallowed hard.

"As long as you don't mind spending fifteen bucks a glass for it."

I winced. It was Lisa and my mother's dime, but the expense account was going to look fishy. "I might as well go for it then."

"I'll send Kikki in with a rum and Coke," he said. "She was in charge of training Broadway."

I was also on vacation and I didn't have to drive anywhere. "Thanks." I unashamedly watched his chiseled ass as he strode out of the room. The quick Google search I did in the parking lot had not prepared me for the sheer force of Miles Carvello in real life. I wouldn't want to piss him off. Apparently, his black belts had black belts. I thought he'd be a thug. I hadn't expected him to be drop-dead sexy.

Kikki sauntered in wearing just a thong and heart-shaped pasties over her nipples. She handed me my drink. I passed her a hundred and twenty and told her to keep the change.

She tucked them expertly into her thong and undulated around the pole. "So, Miles said you wanted to talk to me about Broadway."

"You don't have to dance," I said, kicking my sandals off.

"I want to stay limber," Kikki said, climbing up the pole with lazy circles, using her arm and leg muscles. She made it look easy.

If she thought she was going to shock me, she was in for a big surprise. No one in theater was shy about their bodies. There were too many quick costume changes to worry about things like that.

"So you're Broadway's sister?"

"Yeah." I sipped on the drink. It was slightly stronger than the one from the Spearmint Rhino and had a refreshing twist of lime.

"She didn't talk about her family. She didn't really talk to us at all. I got the feeling she thought she was too good for us."

At least Lisa was consistent. "When was the last time you saw Lisa—Broadway?"

"About three weeks ago." Kikki gripped the bar with the side of her foot and reached down the length of the pole, posing with her arm and leg in an elegant curve.

"Damn, that takes strength," I blurted.

"Thanks," Kikki breathed out, the only sign of strain she gave. She switched positions and straddled the pole. Wrapping her legs around it, Kikki leaned back until she was almost upside down. "Broadway wasn't a pole dancer."

I nodded. After surgery, Lisa wouldn't have had the muscle strength in her leg. I flexed my calves. I wonder if I did?

"She did a good bump and grind, but she wasn't friendly with the customers and acted like she was doing them a favor by dancing on the stage."

That didn't surprise me either.

"Do you know why she wanted to strip?" I asked.

"Money?" Kikki lifted herself up and whirled herself around the pole, kicking her feet. "Don't get me wrong. Some guys like the untouchable ice bitch routine. But not enough that she was in demand."

"She left suddenly without notice. Was it because she wasn't making enough money?"

"Why are you hunting her down, anyway? Are you trying to rescue her from Sin City?" Kikki sneered.

"No, I just want to make sure she's okay and to have her call our mother so she gets off my back."

"That's oddly sweet." Kikki landed with a flourish and took the drink out of my hand and tanked it. That was probably for the best. I needed to keep my head on straight, no matter how much the rest of me wanted to cut loose.

"Do you want a lap dance? You paid for one."

"I'm good, thanks. Take a load off. That was some workout and you made it seem effortless."

Kikki looked surprised. "Most people don't get that."

"Most people didn't take dance lessons for their entire life." When I turned sixteen, I got a job at a convenience store so I could continue my lessons. My mother had thought it was a waste of money, but my dad had convinced her to let me do what I wanted with my meager salary.

"Broadway said she danced professionally. On stage, the real stuff, not just taking off her clothes for money."

"She did. She was really good."

Kikki scowled. "Not that good. She was always icing her leg after a fifteen-minute routine."

"Do you think that's why she stopped stripping?"

"Like I said, we weren't close. When she was here, she did the minimum required and took up space. I was glad to see her go."

"Was there anyone she talked to or got friendly with?"

Kikki got a calculating look in her eye. "I think Mina can help you out."

"Let me guess," I said dryly. "A hundred dollars and a two-drink minimum."

She winked at me and put a lot of jiggle in her wiggle when she walked out.

"Bacardi and Diet Cokes," I called out. Might as well get comfortable. I loosened the belt on my wrap dress and tucked my feet under me on the couch. This could take a while.

CHAPTER FIVE

Miles Carvello

Jackie Mitchell's story checked out, although it took longer than expected. I had Grier run a background search on her and her family. He bitched about it until I told him that I had some pills for him in the safe and another lead in the form of Ginny selling drugs out of Dalton's.

I wrote Jackie's sister's address on a sticky note and went back to the VIP room. I should bring her back to my office, so she wasn't holding up a room for one of the girls. I had wanted to shock her, but that hadn't worked. What had I been thinking? I liked how every emotion flitted across her face. It was intimate sitting there talking to her about stripping. It turned her on and I was one step behind her. If she went back to my office or perhaps upstairs to my apartment, no one would interrupt us.

Rubbing a hand down my face, I needed to get Jackie out of the club before I was tempted to blow off the rest of tonight and show her the town. I should hand her the address and tell her to take her fine New York ass out of my club. When someone ran away from their family to Las Vegas and then disappeared, there was a reason for it. But nothing in Grier's background check convinced me that Lisa Mitchell or her sister were the type to do that sort of thing. It was obvious Jackie was worried that Lisa's disappearance wasn't voluntary, and I knew she wouldn't get anywhere with the cops unless foul play was suspected. So that was why I was breaking privacy rules to give Jackie her sister's address. I knew all about the limitations on police investigations. My uncle's club had been burned down and it had been declared arson, but there hadn't been any convictions.

When I walked into the VIP room, I wasn't expecting Mina to be nursing a rum and Coke on the couch while Jackie was halfway up the stripper pole in her underwear. Holy crap, I was envious of the pole.

Mina shot to her feet and Jackie gave a little shriek and fell on her ass. Good thing the floor was padded.

"Out," I said to Mina, gesturing to the door. She slammed it behind her in her haste to leave. That door was getting a workout tonight.

Jackie sat, splayed out on the floor. Her hair was messy around her face and she hadn't bothered to cover herself. She wore a simple white cotton bra that pushed up her curves enticingly. Her panties covered most of her ass. She looked like an Amish stripper.

"I figured since I was paying premium bucks, I'd get some instruction while I was interviewing your dancers," she said.

My eyes narrowed. Did I detect a slight slurring in her words?

"You thinking about becoming a stripper?" Her damn blush was going to be the death of me.

"Maybe for one night?" Her lips twitched.

Lord help me. I hoisted her up on her feet and considered

kissing her, but figured she'd slap the shit out of me. "You're not the stripper type."

The crazy chick got offended by that.

"I can dance. I'll ace any interview you set up." Jackie glared up at me, her hands on her hips.

"Stripping isn't just dancing. I told you. It's seducing a man out of every dollar bill in his pocket and maxing out his credit card."

Jackie set her shoulders. "I can be seductive."

No shit. But there was seductive and there was taking off your clothes in front of a strange man. I decided to call her bluff. "Show me. If you wow me, I'll let you do a set."

"You'll *let* me strip?" Jackie shook her head in disbelief. "I didn't come here for a job. I came here to find my sister."

"She's not here. Yet, you still are."

"Because the dancers keep stringing me along, feeding me bullshit." She folded her arms in front of her chest. I guess she was mad, but all it did was push up her tits until my mouth almost watered.

"They don't trust you. You're a paycheck to them. Here." I stuck the note on her tempting cleavage and took a reluctant step away from her. I liked being close to her, but she was a distraction that I couldn't afford to indulge in. I had a club to run, and an uncle to avenge. "It's the address she gave on her employment application."

"Thank you," Jackie said warmly and tucked the note into her purse. I expected her to make a beeline out of here or at least get dressed. But she hesitated and looked up at me with her pretty green eyes. "Did you interview her?"

"Yeah." I was wondering if she was going to put her dress back on, but I was enjoying the show too much to point that out to her. My fingers itched to get inside those panties that fit her like a pair of shorts. A bikini would show more skin, but I was enticed by the innocent temptation of her. Jackie wasn't intimidated by being alone with me in her underwear, but that didn't mean she could be an exotic dancer.

"How did she seem?" she asked.

Lisa Mitchell was nothing like her sister. She had been mostly forgettable and a prude. You could tell she didn't like taking her clothes off and was uncomfortable in her own skin. Jackie seemed right at ease and I wanted to feel her body against mine more than I wanted my next breath.

"Miles?"

"Hmm?" I realized I had been staring and forced myself to look away. What the hell had she asked me? Oh yeah. Her sister. "Broadway was a competent dancer, otherwise I wouldn't have hired her."

"Was she strung out or desperate?"

"No. I wouldn't have hired her if she was."

"If I prove to you that I can do this, you said you'd let me do a set. That's not going to be enough."

"Enough for what?" I asked warily.

"Mina said there was one guy who would come in and always ask for Broadway."

"Yeah, that's how it goes. Repeat business." I rubbed by thumb against my fingers, indicating money. "She must have had something he couldn't get enough of."

"Do you think he might show up again? I could hang around and do a few sets. I'd like a chance to talk to him, if he's a regular customer."

"I was joking about the set," I said, staring at her in shock.

"The dancers would warm up to me, if I was one of them." Jackie paced around the room while she spoke.

I didn't like the idea of watching other men drool over her. On the other hand, I'd love for her to dance for me. Privately. "That's not going to work. I need a certain type of dancer."

"I'm a good dancer. I'm better than Lisa. Now, anyway." She muttered the last part under her breath.

"This isn't *A Chorus Line* and you're not in a cattle call for a showgirl position." I gave her a slow once-over. "Although, you've got the legs for it."

"I do?" She smiled as she looked down the line of her legs.

Jackie was going to drive me out of my mind if I didn't put an end to this and her cute exotic dancer fantasies. "You'd freeze the moment it came to take off your clothes." I grinned as her lips tightened. "And my clients want to see more skin. And those granny panties aren't going to cut it on the stage."

"They're not granny panties." Jackie scowled. "You're just used to women in butt floss. Do you know how uncomfortable that is?"

"No, but I'm told you get used to it."

"I don't want to get used to it," she said.

"I can't have full nudes because I'm serving alcohol, but you need to show some tits and ass." Normally, I wouldn't be so crude but the men who came to my club weren't going to be as suave and erudite as I was.

Jackie blushed.

I pointed at her adorable pink cheeks. "And that's why you're not an exotic dancer."

"I'm not ashamed of my body," she said, throwing her arms wide.

"How much have you had to drink?"

Tilting her head, she thought about it. "One at the Spearmint Rhino and one and a half here."

Hmmm, that didn't sound like she was drunk.

"I've been around show people all my life. Everyone is naked backstage, and no one cares. Hell, I've known you all of ten minutes and you don't see me clutching my pearls."

Jackie struck an innocent pose that made me want to see how wicked she could be.

One of us needed a reality check and I wasn't sure which one. "It doesn't matter. I can't contract you to work at Dalton's without a Las Vegas business license and you need to be registered with the Nevada Department of Taxation."

"Did Lisa have all that?"

"Yes."

"That surprises the hell out of me. Lisa had to have her hand held to do her taxes every year and hated filling out forms. She usually just had me do it. I'm surprised she didn't call me up and make me file for her."

"If I had to guess, I'd say because she didn't want to answer any questions."

Jackie murmured something that sounded like she agreed with me. Just when I was about to suggest she get dressed and we could get some dinner, she looked up from nibbling on her damn lip again.

"What happens if I get my license and register with the state?"

"How long are you here for?" Fuck me, but she was serious.

"Two weeks. Less, if I can find her."

"It will take about half that, if you're lucky. You'd be better off working as a subcontractor with one of the other dancers' licenses."

"Could you hire me outright? Like a bartender who dances too."

"If I gave you a salary and let you dance for tips, I'd have a riot on my hands." Wait. Why was I even giving this crazy idea serious thought? Because not only did Jackie Mitchell look mouthwatering in her bra and panties, I also liked talking to her. It had been a hard slog these past two years to get Dalton's to turn a profit. I had to rebuild. Nothing of

Uncle Johnny's Gentlemen's Club had survived the fire. I worked night and day. Sure, there had been women, but no one who lasted longer than two weeks. I was due for another two-week fling and Jackie was clicking all my buttons.

"What if I split the tips amongst all of the staff, not just the dancers? I'm not in this for the money," she said.

I couldn't believe she was still talking about this. I was distracted by the leg lifts she was doing so it took me a full minute to register what she'd just said. "That's already the wrong attitude. Weren't you listening?"

"Yes, but I'm here to find my sister, not hustle for tips. If dancing and sharing tips will get me enough goodwill that people will feel free opening up to me about Lisa, I'm willing to do this."

Was this chick for real? "Are you crazy? No."

"Why?"

"Because you work your ass off in this job. If you're going to do it, you're going to do it right. Your hustle, your tips." *What kind of exotic dancer gives away money? One who has no idea what it's like.* "You're going to earn that money. It's yours. Sure, if you want to tip a few bucks a night to the people who help you like the DJ and the bus staff, that's fine. But no one has the right to that tip money aside from you."

"So are you going to put me on the schedule? If I can get one of the dancers to hire me under their business license, that is. And if I can convince you I'm not going to faint dead away?"

"That's a lot of ifs."

All my dancers were independent business owners. The fifty percent profit split was basically the rent I charged them to dance at Dalton's. I had no doubt that one of them would take a flat nightly fee in exchange for hiring Jackie on as an employee. I had a lot of doubts that they would claim her on taxes or do any official paperwork. But Dalton's was in the clear either way.

"This is a bad fucking idea," I said.

"Why?"

"Because it's messy and complicated. You won't last one night."

"How long did Lisa last?"

"She was so fucking bad, I don't even remember."

"I'm better," Jackie said, but suddenly she didn't sound so sure.

It threw me. She was balls-on, full speed ahead, but when her sister was mentioned it threw her. I definitely didn't need the baggage she was carrying. There was one way to stop this out-of-control train wreck. I'd show her what working the VIP room was all about.

"Let's see what you got." I plopped down on the couch. "Strip."

Jackie froze, her eyes going wide. "So you want me to audition for a part in your show?"

This was going to be fun. I hoped she didn't storm out and would allow me to buy her dinner after this. "I don't have a show. I've got six-hour slots to fill. The bra has got to go, though."

"That could work out. I could look for Lisa during the day, and strip at night."

The crazy chick was considering it and I couldn't believe she wasn't telling me to go to hell.

"Don't you think this is a big sacrifice that you're making for your sister?"

"This isn't even in the top ten of things I've sacrificed for Lisa."

"Why?"

Jackie sighed. "You and my therapist ask the same questions."

"Your therapist owns a titty bar?"

"She could with the money she's made off my family."

"Fair enough." I supposed I didn't have a leg to stand on. I was obsessive about my uncle's murder to the point I'd built a club on top of the ruins of his and worked day and night until it was just as successful as the old place had been. I had done it all to attract the same people who'd approached my uncle. I wanted to know what had been worth killing him and burning his club to the ground. I would do anything for that knowledge. I'd take off my clothes and wiggle my ass if I thought it would get me clues.

"Do you want me to get totally naked?" Jackie asked, breaking me out of my brooding thoughts.

Fuck yeah. "Topless is fine," I said, clearing my throat. "Unless you've got a G-string in that suitcase of a purse."

"You should see my dance bag." Jackie rolled her neck and shoulders. "I wasn't planning on auditioning today."

"This isn't an audition as much as a seduction. Not so much a dance as it is being a salesperson, and the commodity you're selling is your time."

She nodded. "I got it. So if I convince you I'd be a good exotic dancer, you'll let me hang around and ask questions?"

"As long as you work your shift like the other girls and don't piss off my customers." It would never happen, but I was going to have fun watching Jackie's attempt.

"You got a deal," she said, stretching her leg flat up the pole.

My cock twitched. I should stop her. "Music on," I said instead, activating another system command. "Play 'Pour Some Sugar on Me,' by Def Leppard."

The room flooded with the opening lyrics and thundered through the soundproofed room. Jackie narrowed her eyes.

"I looked you up," I said. "You're an entertainment agent. You're a classically trained dancer. This isn't the *Nutcracker*

Suite. You'd be a gorgeous ballerina, but my clients aren't that cultured."

"Music stop," she said.

The sound quit immediately. I tried not to gloat and started to get up. "I wish you luck finding your sister."

"How about something from this century?" Jackie cracked her knuckles and barked out, "Computer, play 'No' by Meghan Trainor."

I barked out a laugh and sat back down. But she wiped the smile off my face when, during the premusic part of the song, she deliberately undid the clasp of her bra and shrugged it slowly off one shoulder then the other. Holy shit, she was serious.

"Jackie are you sober?" I swallowed hard as I caught a glimpse of the top of a dusky pink nipple.

"What happens in Vegas," she said, continuing the slow tease with her bra as she strutted around the room. The entire time she held my eyes in a defiant challenge. My mouth went dry when her bra hit the floor. Her back was to me and she gave me a come-hither look over her shoulder. The sweet line of her back made my fingers itch to touch her.

When the music started, her body pulsed to the music. She lazily twirled around the pole, using it as a prop rather than climbing it. Classically trained or not, she knew how to move her ass and hips. Her natural tits moved up and down to the beat and I couldn't stop the stupid grin that spread over my face.

"They teach you that in ballet school?" I wished I had a pillow to put on my lap to hide how she was affecting me.

"Girl Scouts." She winked, going down to a low crouch and then up again.

"Fuck," I breathed out in a tortured groan.

I was surrounded by half-naked women most days. Aside from a quick appreciation, I didn't really notice it anymore.

But I couldn't take my eyes off Jackie. She danced close, her hips twitching seductively. I leaned forward, stopping myself from reaching for her at the last minute.

Shimmying, she raised her eyebrow.

When I just stared, Jackie strutted back to the pole and swayed her hips against it.

"Are you going to stay all the way over there?"

"Are you going to tip?" She smiled sassily at me.

"It's my club." I said.

She shrugged and mouthed the lyrics at me. "No."

I probably should stop this, but it was too much fun. Reaching into my wallet, I pulled out a twenty-dollar bill. Holding it up between my fingers, I thought she was going to call it off. She stumbled a bit and looked uncertain, but then she tossed her hair, losing herself in the music. Then she dropped into a one-handed plank and did a push-up into some yoga position I barely recognized, before crawling on her hands and knees to me.

"Holy shit," I said hoarsely, the bill dropping to the floor.

She climbed on to the sofa and straddled my lap. I slipped my hands under the elastic of her panties to grab a hold of her sweet ass. Clutching the back of my head, she tugged it back so I was looking at her pretty face instead of at her soft round breasts that were hard and begging to be fondled.

"Are you supposed to touch the dancer?" she asked, swaying to the music

"You can call security if you want." I said and nearly came in my pants when she sank down on my erection and rubbed against it.

Her eyes glazed over in pleasure. Holy crap, this was turning her on. I was going to go off like a rocket. Jackie's fingers dug into my shoulders as she ground herself against me again. We were both breaking Las Vegas decency laws right now if she had been an exotic dancer and I had been her client. But I didn't give a fuck.

I kissed her pouty mouth. She tasted like rum and lime and I wondered if she was sober enough to consent. Reluctantly, I eased back. It was hard to hold my resolve when her eyes remained closed and her lips were still parted. Her hips swayed over me, barely grazing my pants. It was taking all my effort not to thrust up into her. She'd make a fortune on lap dances.

"Jackie." I cleared my throat. "It's getting close to the point of no return here. And I'm about to break my number-one rule."

"Hmm?" she asked, opening her eyes.

The song faded out and the only sound in the VIP room was our rough breathing. I didn't want her to stop, but I could see clarity coming back into her eyes. That and a look of horrified disbelief.

"What's your number-one rule?" she whispered.

"No fucking in the VIP room," I said hoarsely. "You got your shot on stage."

CHAPTER SIX

Jackie Mitchell

What the absolute fuck just happened? It felt naughty, but oh so right. I touched my kiss-swollen lips. That was a hell of a dance, one that could have quickly gone nuclear. I had stumbled off him and gotten dressed, not daring to look him in the eye. All he would have had to do was crook his little finger and I'd be back in his lap. I wasn't sure what would be worse —if he had or if he'd just shrugged off the experience. Things like that probably happened to him every day. Things like that only happened to *me* in Las Vegas.

Vegas was a temptation. Especially for someone like me. I'd spent most of my life denying myself for others—mostly my sister. I hadn't been in town twenty-four hours before the reckless feeling of freedom led me into a hot time with a sexy stranger. The erotic haze faded as the cool air-conditioning in the rental car kicked in. My face was on fire, and my body kept playing back how Miles felt underneath me. I'd rubbed myself all over his hard muscles. I squirmed a bit and let out a small sigh. It hadn't been enough, and I really wanted more with him.

I would never be able to do that with a paying customer. Or could I?

Catching a glimpse of myself in the rearview mirror, I looked flushed and a little wild. That wasn't me. But maybe it was. The last time this had happened, I blamed all the shots we did. I wound up dancing in a bar that had suspended bird cages sized for adults. And then I took a bouncer home for the weekend.

"I have a type," I said aloud. The GPS piped up that I needed to turn left and the destination would be on my right.

If I was going to become a stripper this week, type didn't matter. According to Miles and the other dancers I'd spoken with, the only thing that mattered was the money. Lisa hadn't hustled and they had hated her for it. I needed the dancers at Dalton's to accept me so that I could figure out what went wrong with Lisa and maybe get a few clues as to where she went next. But I didn't want to be intimate with strangers I wasn't attracted to. I doubted Miles would pay me for a lap dance every night—not that I wanted him to. For him, I'd do it for free.

I was willing to dance on stage and do a striptease. I wasn't ashamed of my body. I had trained hard even when being a professional dancer was out of the question, because in the back of my mind, I knew that I would audition for a show again. Unfortunately between the pressure of school, work, and Lisa those auditions had been few and far between. It had taken Lisa's accident to slow down both of our lives. And while I felt no guilt about finally taking my shot, I knew I couldn't do it if my sister needed me. But there were limits to my devotion.

There was no way I was going to bump and grind on a guy that looked more like Jason Voorhees than Jason Momoa. I wasn't in this for the money. I needed to find Lisa before my vacation time ran out. There had to be a way to compromise so that I could avoid the VIP room and stick to just the stage.

When the GPS said I'd reached my destination, I found a place to park on the side of the road and hoped I wouldn't get a ticket. I stared up at the lackluster apartment building. It was in a part of town that was crowded with people from all walks of life, reminding me a little of Brooklyn. Lisa would fit right in. Why had she come to Las Vegas of all places, though? If she had wanted to get as far away from my mother as possible, she could have gone to California or Hawaii.

Still, I understood the lure of Sin City.

Groaning, I pressed my forehead to the steering wheel. How did trying to find Lisa evolve into me taking off my clothes and dancing? I had to admit, it excited me a bit. Was this how Lisa felt? Was it the thrill of the forbidden that tempted her to throw off the strict rules and regulations she'd made for herself? Or did she want to dance again and feel the approval of the crowd without straining her knee? And then there was the money. I couldn't shake the allure of making so much in such a short time.

I checked my phone again. Why wasn't she answering my calls? I could understand her ditching Mom, but Lisa had to know by now that I would go away and leave her alone once she checked in. Getting out of the car, I locked it up. *Please be home.*

At the building's entrance, I rang the bell under her apartment number, but there wasn't an answer. It was just past eleven. I should have waited until the morning. If she had a day job, she'd be getting ready for bed. If she had a night job, she'd be working. I waited a few moments and buzzed again. Still nothing. I didn't want to come back tomorrow. I wanted to see her or at least see her apartment tonight. While I was debating what to do, an older gentlemen exited the building and he held the door open for me.

"Thank you," I said.

Lisa's apartment was on the ground floor, so I walked down the hall and knocked on her door. I hoped she'd answer and let me inside. We'd have a glass of wine and I'd be reassured that she was just fine and was hiding out in Sin City from our family and her responsibilities. I'd wish her well and spend the rest of the week doing touristy things and convincing myself not to go back to Dalton's and Miles Carvello.

The door flung open and a woman—not Lisa—glared at me. She wore a half tied robe. "What?"

"I'm Lisa's sister," I said.

"She doesn't live here anymore." The woman started to close the door.

"Wait," I said, grabbing the door. "Do you know where she is or how I can find her?"

"No. She left in a hurry and put me in a bad spot for next month's rent."

"I can pay her part of the rent for this month, if you can spare a few moments to talk with me."

The woman glared suspiciously. "How did you get this address?"

"Miles Carvello gave it to me."

Her face cleared. "Oh." She opened the door wide. "Come on in. This should be good."

"I'm sorry for bothering you."

"I should have been up anyway. I've got to go to work in a couple of hours." She stifled a yawn behind her hand. "I'm Becka, by the way. Your sister left me high and dry for five hundred dollars."

"I can write you a check or wire it into your account."

Becka thought about it and said, "Can you PayPal it?"

Once I sent it, Becka brightened up a bit. "Would you like a cup of coffee?"

"Thanks," I said, although drinking coffee at this time a night would guarantee I'd be up for hours. I pushed Miles Carvello and what we could do to pass time out of my mind. Scanning the small living area, I didn't see a trace of Lisa. "Was that her room?" I pointed to the closed door.

"Yeah. Feel free to look around, but she took all of her stuff out."

Inside the small bedroom was a generic futon bed that had seen better days, an Ikea night table, and an empty closet with a beaded curtain. It looked like my college dorm room. I did a quick search of the room, but I didn't even see so much as a dust bunny. Going back into the main room, I sat down at the kitchen table.

"How long did Lisa live here?"

"This would have been her third month."

The timing seemed right. "How did you two meet?"

Becka handed me a cup of coffee and then sat down across from me with one of her own. "We met at a job interview for a cocktail waitress at the New York-New York casino. I said I had a room for rent. She paid me cash for the first month. That was good enough for me. I wound up getting the job. She went on to work at the Spearmint Rhino."

"She doesn't work there anymore. Do you know where she's working now?"

"If Miles gave you this address, then you know she was stripping at Dalton's."

I nodded. "But she left a few weeks ago. There was a man at the club that came in to see her sometimes. One of the dancers told me he was an older guy. White hair, short beard? Did she ever talk about him or bring him around?"

Becka frowned and shook her head. "She never had anyone over, and I don't remember her talking about a guy."

"What reason did she give you for moving out so suddenly?"

"She said she got a gig that included room and board." Becka looked into her cup of coffee, then back up at me.

"Like a hospitality job. Maybe for one of the hotels around here?"

"She wouldn't tell me. I got the impression that it was a more . . . private contract."

I felt an icy chill. "Do you think it was sex work?"

"Why? Because all strippers are hookers?" Becka snapped.

"No." But it had crossed my mind. If Lisa was willing to strip for quick cash, she could have also convinced herself that she could sell her body to pay off her medical bills. It didn't sound so farfetched. Lisa hated owing anything to anybody. She was the only person I knew who didn't have any credit card debt or student loans. "But it would account for why she hasn't contacted us in two weeks and has been super secretive. Did she ever say why she came to Vegas?"

"She said she wanted a change of scenery and she was sick of the New York winters. She might have mentioned that her family was a little clingy. You look like her, now that I'm more awake."

"I do?" No one had ever said that to me before.

"Same eyes. Same expressions. Why are you here?"

"My parents are terrified something happened to her."

"So why aren't they here? Why did they send you?"

I shrugged. "It's what I do."

"Maybe Lisa isn't the only one who needs a change of scene."

I thought briefly about Miles. "Vegas does have a certain charm."

"That goes away after you live here for a while. I don't

know where she's working now or why she'd leave. She had a good deal at Dalton's."

"In what way?"

"How well do you know Miles?"

"I don't really." Although, he knew a lot about me from that little dance that I did. I fought a blush, but Becka noticed it.

"He's sex on a stick, isn't he? I used to work for him. He's one of the good guys and takes care of his employees. He's at that club twenty-four seven and knows what's going down there. Lisa wouldn't have left unless she got a better deal with someone she trusted."

"Is that why you left?"

"I got sick of the groping and the cheap-ass tippers. At least with waitressing you only have to put up with an ass pinch and a stray hand here and there, and the tips are just as good."

"As good as the VIP room?"

She barked out a quick laugh. "No. I do miss that part. The money. Not the men."

"Did Lisa feel uncomfortable with it?"

Shrugging, Becka lit up a cigarette. I tried not to make a face. I hated the smell, but it was her house. "She liked the money."

"You don't have any idea where she went or why?" She'd already said she didn't, but I was hoping for a different answer.

"I wish I did. Like I said, she owed me rent."

"I'm at a dead end following my sister's trail. The only thing I was able to find out from the dancers at Dalton's was about that recurring customer I mentioned. I'm going to strip there this week to try and find out where she might have gone."

Becka smiled. "You'd do that for your sister?"

If I was being honest, I was doing it for me too. I had wanted to dance on the stage and now was my chance. Of course, the men at the club weren't buying tickets to see my *Cabaret* number. But the thought of being watched and an object of desire was appealing, and part of me wanted to see the lust in Miles Carvello's eyes again.

"Once I get an exotic dancer to let me subcontract with them."

"I'll hire you for a small weekly fee."

"How small?"

Becka thought about it. "A hundred dollars a week. Pay me the first week right now and I'll send the paperwork over to Dalton's tomorrow."

"You got a deal." I shook her hand and handed her a hundred from my rapidly dwindling pile. I hadn't been in Vegas a full day and I already spent half the money my mother gave me.

"Why do think dancing at Dalton's will help find your sister?"

"I'm hoping her mystery man will come back and I can ask him some questions. Maybe Lisa will show up." I shrugged. "I've got two weeks before I have to get back home. I'll be able to gather more clues at Dalton's than I will in my hotel room."

"Just be careful," Becka said. "Miles and his security team are the best, but even they can't be everywhere. That part of town isn't the greatest and if it's not gang problems, it's the drugs."

"Was Lisa using?" I didn't think she was. If I hadn't taken her to get her stomach pumped, I would never even had asked.

"She had a full prescription of oxy, but I think that was just for her knee."

If she was taking opioids for the pain, there was something really wrong. When she was working, it had been hard enough to get Lisa to take an aspirin.

"Was there anything out of the ordinary going on with her in the days leading up to her moving out?"

"I'm sorry I'm not more help," Becka said. "We both worked nights and kept to ourselves. We shared a meal or two and hung out with drinks in front of the television a few days a week, but we weren't close. I did get the feeling that she was very unhappy and was trying everything she could think of not to be."

"Did she ever mention money issues?"

"No."

"Did she leave a forwarding address?"

"No."

I pushed down the frustration. It wasn't Becka's fault that Lisa was Lisa. It just made me crazy. Reaching into my purse, I handed her my business card. "If you can think of anything else, please give me a call. And if you see Lisa, tell her we're worried, and a quick phone call would go a long way."

"I will," Becka said. "And maybe I'll come by and check out your gig at Dalton's."

"You better be a good tipper," I said.

CHAPTER SEVEN

Miles Carvello

I deliberately scheduled Jackie for the shit shift, noon to six p.m. It would very nearly guarantee that she'd have a hard time booking a VIP lounge or a lap dance. Even though it was a Friday, things didn't get going until later. Unless she was aggressive, she'd collect the tips from the horndogs around the stage and escape their greedy hands mostly unscathed. I wasn't sure why I cared so much, but the thought of someone else's hands on her soft skin made me want to punch something.

Of course, I hadn't counted on Chance and the bachelor party to come in this early. And it figured that they now took up the entire first row around the stage she was going to use. They ordered beers and tipped the waitress a fifty to keep them supplied.

"For someone who's going to make a killing on liquor this month, you're not looking too happy," Highway said, leaning up against the support pole so he could watch both the door and the stage.

"Don't you have anything better to do?" I growled.

"I want to see the new girl."

That was the problem. Everyone did. During her orientation yesterday, I tried to stay as far away as possible from Jackie. But it hadn't worked out so well. Mav had said I hovered like a helicopter mom and Kikki remarked that I'd never watched the girls warm up before. The only saving grace was that Jackie looked as distracted by me as I was by her. In the end, I told myself to find something to do in my office or nothing would get done while she and I eye fucked each other.

But of course everyone noticed and it caused more buzz than I would have liked to have given a newly minted stripper. My off-duty staff was here anyway, working the bachelor party, doing lap dances and keeping the Aussies happy. That should have pissed off the on-duty staff, but curiosity was a great equalizer. Everyone was positioned to see the stage, like sharks scenting blood in the ocean. They were going to make her first dance hell and I hoped it scared her off. Jackie Mitchell shouldn't have to strip because her sister was an inconsiderate bitch.

"What name did she pick?" Highway asked.

"La Vie Bohème. It's also the name of the song she's dancing to now." The somber strains of the song from the musical *Rent* started, and Jackie slowly strutted out wrapped in what looked like a thousand scarves. She'd told me she spent most of the day yesterday shopping for costumes.

"This sounds like a dud." Highway frowned as the tempo slightly increased. Every time the chorus of the song said, "La Vie Bohème," Jackie did a hip bump and a scarf fell to the floor.

"It picks up," I said.

"She knows they're not here to see a ballet, right?" he said as Jackie went up on her toe and spun like a ballerina in a music box.

"Just wait." Jackie had run the concept by him, but hadn't actually rehearsed the song in front of anyone at the club, which was another reason why it was standing room only out here.

As the lyrics got more suggestive, her hips went wild and the scarves flew in all directions until Jackie was left just wearing pasties over her nipples and hot red booty shorts. She acted out the voice parts, getting the audience involved. She was a natural and a damn good dancer. She leapt and twirled around the pole and it looked like she was floating.

"Are you sure she's never done this before?" Highway squinted at Jackie.

"To S&M," she sang with the music, flinging her arms wide.

The Aussies roared and jumped to their feet.

"Holy shit," Highway croaked.

Jackie slid around like a snake on the stage, accepting bills into the waistband of her shorts. Then she coiled away and slowly sauntered off the stage as the song wound down.

"That was a hell of a way to warm up the room." Highway said, and went back to his post by the door.

She killed it. I hid a grin behind my hand, ridiculously proud of her. I noticed that some of the dancers weren't so happy that Jackie had made such a splash on her first number. But they were reaping the benefits of the excited audience. Kikki and Mina took two of the bachelor party guys into the VIP room. Chance was all in, dancing by his chair this time, to Nalia's gyrations to J Lo and Pitbull's "On the Floor."

"Make sure Chance stays off the stage tonight," I ordered Mav over the headset.

Making my way back to the kitchen, I saw that we were a

little short staffed, so I put a load of bar glasses into the dishwasher. "Where is everyone?" I asked Liu, my chef.

"Paulie is a no-show. No answer at his house." Paulie was the dishwasher. "Dee hasn't been into work for two days. Her mother hasn't seen her." Dee was his sous chef. "And Zeke's phone has been disconnected." Zeke was a waiter.

"What the actual fuck?" *Was someone stalking my staff, discouraging them from coming to work?*

"Something in the water," Liu grunted as he took stock of the supplies. "I need some help."

"What can I do?"

Liu gave me a dismissive look. "You can stay the hell out of my kitchen. Go knock heads together and let me create."

I rolled my eyes. He made the best damn appetizers I'd ever tasted, and he did it cheap and made a ton of food. He kept me in the black almost as much as the liquor sales did and he knew it.

"Then what do you need?" I wondered where I'd` put the number of that temp agency I used when the shit hit the fan.

"I've got my cousins coming in. You're going to pay them under the table for tonight."

I grunted. Not the way I wanted to do business, but I didn't want a bunch of hungry, angry customers either. "They want permanent jobs?"

"They've misplaced their social security cards."

Plugging my fingers in my ears, I said, "I don't want to know about that."

"Cash at three a.m."

"Fine. But just for tonight."

I pushed thoughts of the legality of my kitchen staff tonight out of my mind for the moment. Liu would handle it. What the heck was going on? Like any bar in a tourist town, we had turnover, but most people gave notice or at least the courtesy of a phone call. Zeke, Paulie, and Dee had been at

Dalton's for over a year. For all three of them not to come in tonight was suspicious. And if Dee hadn't checked in for two days, something was up.

I went into the employee break room and glared at the missing staff's lockers. They knew that I could search their lockers at any time. It was in their employee contract, but I hated doing it.

"Mav," I said over the headset. "Can you ask around and see if anyone's heard from Zeke, Paulie, or Dee?" A thought hit me and I didn't like it. "See if you can find out how friendly they were with Ginny or Broadway."

People moved on from Vegas all the time. They also got in trouble. Three people not answering their phones was suspicious. Four, if you counted Jackie's sister. I remembered Ginny's threats to me and suddenly they didn't seem so silly.

I cut the lock off of Zeke's locker first. He had a change of clothes and a pair of sneakers that could use a wash or at least a good dousing with Febreze. I found a carton of cigarettes, an unopened pack of condoms, and about fifty one-dollar bills. But I didn't see any clues on why he had bailed on us. Or signs that he was leaving for good. He would have at least taken the cash and the cigarettes.

Dee's locker was completely empty. I knew for a fact she kept an extra chef's jacket and a change of clothes to change into after shift. So maybe Dee knew she wasn't coming back. But for her not to tell Liu didn't make any sense.

I hit the jackpot with Paulie's locker. A large plastic baggie of marijuana, a smaller one of pills, and a pistol. He also wouldn't have left this behind if he'd cut and run. The pistol was loaded.

"Stupid," I muttered and unloaded it. I put the magazine into my pocket and the pistol into my pants in the center of my back. I stuffed the drugs into a fast food bag I found in the trash and hurried through the club to secure the drugs and the gun in the safe in my office. Grier was coming tomorrow and hopefully he'd have some insight on what was going on.

It was a coincidence that I was back on the floor when Jackie's second number came up. At least, that was what I told myself. She was in thigh-high, white-studded leather boots, with a matching cap and jacket. I could see flashes of her breasts inside the coat as she stomped and shook her hips to "Does Your Mother Know" from the movie *Mamma Mia*. She must have tipped the DJ, because Javi put the strobes up all over her so they caught the silver studs on the jacket and cap.

She knew how to work the room. Her joy at being up there was infectious. Because she was sincerely having fun, so was everyone else. Most strippers played the crowd with vacant looks or practiced leers. Jackie was singing along to the music and entertaining the crowd, flirting outrageously. She had a way of making the man she looked at think he was the only one in the room. I was too far away for her to see me, but I had a bird's-eye view of the spell she was weaving over the jaded crowd. Fresh and new, with a splash of youthful innocence, she was a big hit with the bachelor party.

And the way she moved her body sent mine into overdrive.

I didn't date strippers. It wasn't a rule. It was just good business sense. I was a shitty boyfriend because I was always working. But she wasn't going to be here very long, and I couldn't come up with a reason why I couldn't be in Jackie's bed tonight, especially if she was as eager to grind on me as she was last night.

The jacket came off and her perky breasts jiggled free. She wore shiny pasties that sparkled in the flashing lights as she high kicked and threw herself into the music with her entire body. She used the pole as a dance partner, but I could see a few of Kiki's moves when she twirled around. Jackie was a fast learner.

She put her cap on Chance's head and shimmied her chest at him.

Mav was already there to put a restraining hand on his shoulder when Chance would have joined Jackie on the stage. Her hands went to the studded belt she wore. She snapped it free of the loops and her shorts fell to her ankles. She was wearing butt floss. My cock nearly jumped up and cheered. Then she kicked her shorts away and ended her song in a deep split.

My mouth dropped open. If I had any business sense, I'd switch her to the prime-time slots. But I wanted to keep her all to myself.

Chance held up his credit card. "To the VIP room."

My hands clenched into fists as Jackie took his hand after wrapping the belt over his shoulders. It was only Highway's hand on my shoulder that stopped me from following.

"Not a good idea, boss."

I thought it was a fucking *great* idea.

"Did you know that Paulie was selling drugs out of the club?" I asked instead.

Highway frowned. "I never saw anything, but it makes sense."

"Why?"

"I couldn't figure out why Ginny was fucking that little prick."

Paulie was the supplier. I had a solid lead for Grier. "What about Dee or Zeke?"

"They weren't fucking Paulie."

I supposed that was information that was important to someone. "Do you think they were selling to him or buying from him or Ginny?"

"I don't think so. They did hang out with the dancers after their shifts."

"Which ones?"

"The ones who had a side business after hours."

I snorted. That wasn't drugs. That was sex. I didn't care what the dancers did when they were off the clock and off my property, as long as it didn't affect their jobs when they were on stage.

"Did they hang around with Broadway?"

"Zeke did. He was the only one who liked her. I don't think she let him fuck her though."

Holding up a hand, I said, "I don't care who is fucking who. What I want to know is what's going on with my employees. They're dropping like flies."

"Shit happens."

I couldn't argue with that. My eyes slid over to the closed VIP door where Jackie and Chance had gone. "Has it been fifteen minutes yet?"

"No, but Chance paid for an hour."

"What?" I whipped my head to Highway. "How the fuck do you know that?"

He tapped his headset. "I heard her call it in. His card went through."

I usually didn't need to be on the headset until later in the evening so I hadn't turned on my Bluetooth. "That son of a bitch spent four hundred dollars on Jackie?"

"La Vie Bohème," Highway corrected me. "More like five twenty after the booze."

I forced my jaw to unclench.

"And that's not including tip," he added helpfully.

"Fuck."

"You shouldn't get involved with strippers, boss. They'll break your balls, your heart, and your bank account. And not necessarily in that order."

Just what I needed, love advice from my head bouncer. "Look, just ask around and keep your ears open. Find out everything you can about Paulie, Dee, and Zeke—especially if it has to do with Broadway. I don't think Broadway's white haired friend is going to come back."

"Where are you going?" Highway asked.

"My office," I snarled. If Zeke and Broadway met up outside of work, he might know where she was. Or if I was really lucky, Lisa would be with him and her sister could get off the stage and away from Chance fucking Bateman. I had some calls to make.

CHAPTER EIGHT

Jackie Mitchell

I tried not to flinch as the door shut behind me. I carried in a bottle of Jose Cuervo and a tray with ice, glasses, salt, and lemons. My mind could barely tally what I was going to make this hour. It was at least two hundred dollars and I knew I got a cut when the client ordered premium booze. That wasn't counting the fifty bucks I had already made in tips tonight.

Or the tip Chance Bateman might leave me. Oh my God, Lisa would shit if she knew.

"Poor me a drink, would ya luv?" he said in a sexy Australian accent.

"S-sorry," I said, hurrying to put the tray down on the table.

"Join me in a shot?"

"Yeah," I said.

He licked his hand and I dotted the salt on it. I filled the shot glass with the Cuervo. Sucking the salt off his hand, he then tanked the shot and I popped the lemon wedge into his mouth. He grinned, showing me the rind of the lemon over his teeth.

I laughed at his antics and relaxed a bit.

"Your turn," he said. "You look like you could use one."

"It's my first night." I licked my hand and blushed at his appreciative look.

"No shit."

"Is it that obvious?"

"Only because you haven't sat on my lap yet."

I nearly dropped the shot I had just poured myself. "Am I supposed to?"

"Not if you don't want to," he said with a smile, and took the shot out of my hand and tanked it.

"I don't think that's how it works," I said, reluctantly. I handed him a lemon slice, but he waved me off.

"It is with me. But I *am* going to make you pour me a real drink."

I couldn't believe how relieved I was to hear him say that, and I quickly blinked back tears so he wouldn't see. My bravado that had gotten me this far was rapidly fading away as the adrenaline from being on stage wore off. Chance Bateman was hotter than the sun, and was even more attractive because he was kind and funny. But I didn't want to grind on his lap. I didn't mind being nearly naked in front of him, mostly because he wasn't leering, and his admiration was a confidence builder. But there was only one man I wanted to rub against in the VIP room, and he probably was busy in the club making sure no one was out of line. "How would you like your drink?" I asked.

"On the rocks with a salted rim and a twist of lemon."

I figured out how to create that, and handed it to him.

"Feel free to make yourself one."

Looking at the tequila bottle longingly, I sighed. "If you want me to dance, I shouldn't."

"Are you okay with dancing?"

"I love it." I felt the last of my nervousness slip away. Chance didn't turn me on, but he made me feel safe.

Leaning back into the couch, he waved at me to start.

"Music on," I said. "Play 'Baby Did a Bad, Bad Thing' by Chris Isaak."

"Good choice." He crossed his legs and winced. It reminded me of Lisa. Chance must have hurt his knee at some point.

I lost myself in the music, using the entire room to dance, leap, and shimmy. It should have been tawdry, and I should have been embarrassed that I was, for all intents and purposes, naked with a strange man. But I wasn't. When I looked over, Chance was smiling at me, content to watch. Considering all the times I'd stared at his ass on Lisa's poster, it felt like turnabout was fair play.

He even clapped for me when the song was done. I gave him my best diva bow. A deep curtsy where I pretended I had a large bouquet of roses in my arms.

"Have a drink and a seat. You deserve it."

"I do," I agreed. "Let me refresh yours."

"That's a good girl," he said with that sexy accent, flirting with a smoldering look through impossibly long lashes.

It was the same one from his calendar and I couldn't help grinning back.

After I fixed our drinks, I joined him on the couch. He turned to face me, and I tried not to think about yesterday when Miles and I almost broke rule number one. I shoved down the disappointment that we hadn't.

"I've got to know," Chance began.

"What's a nice girl like me doing in a place like this?" I finished.

"Don't get me wrong," he said. "Dalton's is one of my

favorite titty bars and I love Miles like a brother. He saved my life."

"He did?"

"I was about to get beaned with a beer bottle and Miles took it on his forearm instead. Ten stitches."

"Wow," I said. "He's like Superman."

"I wouldn't go that far," Chance said. "But he's a good bloke to have on your side in a fight."

"I'm here looking for my sister, Lisa."

Chance made a show of looking around. "I don't see her. But I've got plenty of credit left on my card if she shows up. Sisters." He waggled his eyebrows at me.

I couldn't help but laugh, but I had to look away.

"What's wrong, luv?"

"I wish I could invite her to join us. She's a huge fan. I've seen you in a towel many times."

He grimaced. "I'm embarrassed."

"Don't be. You have a really nice smile."

Chance barked out a laugh. "Hey, that's my line."

"And you've got a great ass."

He clinked his glass with mine. "Right back atcha. So where is your sister?"

His accent made it sound like *sis-tah*.

"I wish I knew. The last anyone saw her was here about three weeks ago. She doesn't answer my or our parents' calls. She moved out of her apartment in New York after her ACL surgery."

"Fuck." Chance got very still. "She was an athlete?"

"Lead dancer on Broadway. Her whole life ended when they told her she couldn't dance again."

Chance stared down into his drink and swirled the ice around, a pensive look on his face.

"She came to Vegas. First as a bartender, then as a strip-per. But I think her leg gave out. I tracked her to her apartment, but she left her roommate in the lurch. The only clues I've got to go on are that she told her roommate she'd found a job with room and board, and there was a guy who came to Dalton's to see her a few times."

Chance leaned forward. "So you decided to become a stripper to see if that guy comes back?"

"That and maybe if the other dancers start to trust me, they'll remember something about Lisa. Some clue that will help me find her. I was more pissed than worried when I came down here. But now I'm wondering if my mother wasn't overreacting after all."

"How long are you planning on staying?"

"I've got another week before I have to go back to New York."

"New Yawk," he teased.

"You're going to talk about *my* accent?"

"Tawk."

I rolled my eyes. "Do you want me to dance again?"

"If you want," he said.

He had to be the easiest client I would ever get. I wanted to make sure he got his money worth. "Music on. 'Bad Things' by Jace Everett."

"The *True Blood* theme song. I loved that show."

"The books were better," I said as I started the routine.

"They always are." He watched me for a while. "I'm guessing you're a Broadway dancer too?"

My chest swelled with pride that he thought I was talented enough to be on Broadway. Chance Bateman was good for my ego. He was going to ruin me for all other clients. "Not yet. I'm Lisa's manager."

"You're talented."

"Lisa's better," I said, like I always did.

"Not anymore," he said, and the bitterness in his voice threw me off my rhythm. But his face almost immediately cleared, and I wondered if I'd imagined it. I finished the song more out of breath than I thought I'd be. I was starting to feel a twinge in my calves. I wasn't used to dancing like this.

"We're here for the rest of the week too," Chance said, sipping his drink. "Why don't I help you look for your sister?"

"You'd do that?" I gaped at him.

"We're planning on hitting every bar and strip club in Nevada. Some places will be a bit unsavory. I might as well keep an eye out for her. Lisa is her name?"

"Lisa Mitchell. Her stripper name is Broadway. If you give me your phone, I'll bring up her portfolio so you can see what she looks like."

"What's your name, my little bohemian?"

"Jackie," I said. "Jackie Mitchell." I brought up the Zimmerman website and clicked over to Lisa's headshot and biography.

"It's nice to meet you, Jackie."

"Nice to meet you too." I ducked my head, suddenly shy. I handed him back his phone. "That's her."

Chance studied the picture. "I haven't seen her so far."

"How can you be sure?"

"I never forget a pretty face."

He really was a charmer. If I hadn't imprinted on Miles and the burly bouncer type I could see myself falling for Chance's smile and roguish good looks.

I took his phone back and typed my cell number into his address book. "Here's my number. Call me day or night if you see her."

"No worries. If she's in Vegas and out in public, we'll find her."

"Why are you doing this?" He didn't seem like he was working an angle.

"I've got a sister who runs a little wild too. Her name's

Adele. If she went missing in a town like this, I'd be going crazy."

I bit my lip and looked away. "I'm going to hit all the hotels on the Strip and all the ones that give room and board to their employees."

"That last is going to be a short list," Chance said gently.

"That's what I'm afraid of." I needed to start another dance otherwise the thought of my sister prostituting herself would choke me. I would have helped her financially, but she wouldn't have accepted it. I never thought she'd choose to sell her body though. Maybe she hadn't. But I couldn't think of another job that would provide room and board in Vegas.

"I could check out some of the chicken ranches," Chance offered.

"Oh, she doesn't like farms."

Chance coughed to hide a laugh. "Chicken ranch is another name for brothel."

My face was probably neon red. I hadn't heard that term before. "Very altruistic of you to check those out for me," I said, getting up to pace the room. I went through songs I liked in my head, so I could find one to dance to so I could lose myself in the dance again.

He put a hand over his heart. "I'm willing to sacrifice to aid a damsel in distress."

"You are a prince among men."

"Most people think I'm a cocky bastard. Besides," he said sobering. "We responsible siblings have to stick together. If I could save you the heartache I would. Sometimes I wish I could wrap Adele in bubble wrap, so she doesn't get hurt."

"You're a good brother."

"Not really," he said. "But I'm trying."

"Do you have any requests?" I asked, twirling around the pole.

"Music on," he said. "Play 'You Can Leave Your Hat On.'" He tossed me my white leather cap.

I spent the rest of the hour trading dances with him and sipping tequila. He was a good dancer and really rocked Beyonce's "Crazy in Love." I pretended not to notice his slight limp and, at the end of the hour, he poured himself a large glass of tequila and rubbed his knee.

"Be a luv and send in Maya for me, will you?"

I nodded. "Thanks for everything, Chance. You were my first and I'll never forget you."

He pretended to leer at me. "You can stay if you want and I'll show you some more firsts."

"I can't keep all of this," I waved my hand up and down his body, "to myself. That would be selfish."

"There's enough of me to go around." He winked. "We'll find your sister."

I had to get out of here before I started to cry again. I nodded and opened the door. And nearly walked smack into a man's chest.

"Miles," I said in surprise when he cupped my elbow. "I need to get Maya."

Miles pressed a button on his earpiece. "Maya to room three," he barked.

"Everything okay, mate?" Chance asked from inside the room, looking at the two of us curiously.

Miles pulled me closer to him. "Maya will be right with you."

Chance raised his glass to us. I gave him a quick wave before Miles whisked me down a corridor and into a large office. He closed the door behind us.

"Is something wrong?"

Miles whirled to face me. He was really close. I took a step back and hit the solid wood of the door. He placed his hands on the door next to my head. The heat coming off him singed my skin. And for the first time in an hour I remembered I was naked except for two stickers on my nipples and a frothy piece of string and beads that barely covered my lady bits.

"How was it?" he rasped.

I swallowed hard. An hour with Chance and I wasn't even a little bit aroused. Two seconds alone with Miles and I was dying for him to rest his hard body against me. Heat and menace radiated off him in waves. He was blocking me from leaving and I was afraid if he didn't move I was going to embarrass myself by kissing him silly.

"My calves are killing me," I said and looked down at my leg, hoping he'd inch back and look too. No dice.

"You were incredible. Top-notch."

I flushed. My heart pounded. He liked it. He liked my dancing.

"You're fired."

"What?" I shrieked. "Why?"

"I'm not spending another hour like the last one."

"What are you talking about?"

He kissed me. He tasted like mint and whiskey and I must have tasted like lemon and tequila, but it worked. It was like he threw a lit match into a puddle of gasoline. I went up in flames. I started tearing at his shirt, but I didn't want to stop kissing him long enough to take it off. So I slid my hands underneath it, reveling in the strong plane of his stomach and the powerful muscles of his back.

Plucking the pasties off my nipples, Miles groaned in satisfaction. He cupped my breasts in his hands while his mouth continued to savage mine. Our tongues dueled, sliding around and exploring. I leaned into his rough caresses that were driving the fever pitch of lust washing over me. Unbuttoning his jeans, I yanked them down his narrow hips. His erection pressed into my belly as we hit the door hard.

I rubbed up and down his body as he kicked off his jeans. The fragile G-string snapped apart with one strong yank and the beaded confection shredded. Before I could hook my leg around his waist, Miles thrust two fingers inside me. I screamed into his mouth at the sudden flare of pleasure. Grabbing onto his shoulders for balance, I felt all strength drain from my legs as he continued to torture my clit with fast strokes. I was so wet, I could hear the slippery sound of his fingers moving though me. Whimpering, I danced on them. I wanted to come again, just as lighting fast as the first time, but the bastard was teasing me.

Tangling my fingers in his hair, I moaned into his mouth. We hadn't stopped kissing and I would gladly give up breathing to keep this feeling going. But he pulled away and looked at me with burning eyes.

"I'm going to fuck you."

"Yes," I breathed.

"I'd like to take my time, but I can't."

"Okay." His fingers played me like a guitar.

He dipped his head to my breasts and sucked hard on my nipple. It pushed me over the edge, and I crested into another limb-shaking orgasm. Miles put his fingers into his mouth and sucked on them. It was so erotic I started to go to my knees. I wanted to drive him as crazy as he was driving me. But he pulled me up and tossed me toward his desk. I splayed facedown across it.

"Condom," I managed to gasp out.

"Of course," he said, spreading my legs wide. And then he was sucking on my pussy. I shrieked in surprise at the erotic pleasure of it. His fingers held me open while his tongue explored my slick folds like it had my mouth.

"Miles!" His tongue penetrated me only to go back to licking me to another orgasm. I was going to die of pleasure. It was all I could do to keep breathing as Miles made sure I was a sopping wet mess. Every erotic feeling that had pulsed through me while I was dancing tonight came to the forefront and I gave in to them now. It was decadent and addicting and I wanted more and more. When he'd wrung every last shiver and tremor out of me, he left me there wide open and waiting. I was dimly aware of the crinkle of foil and his satisfied hiss before his strong hands clamped on my hips and held me still while he drove deep inside.

I screamed, grabbed the desk, and violently bucked to meet each thrust of his powerful body. Lights flashed before my eyes and for a moment I was back on the stage dancing. My nipples scraped against the top of his desk and I stood up on my toes so I wouldn't miss a delicious stroke.

"Jackie," he groaned "I've been thinking about doing this ever since our lap dance.

"Me too," I panted.

I wanted him to fuck me hard and fast to another explosion. Dancing had turned me on tonight. I'd had fun with Chance, but being here with Miles fulfilled every fantasy. I loved Las Vegas. I loved this feeling of freedom and losing every inhibition that had held me back while I was in Lisa's shadow in New York.

"Miles," I begged, straining toward the glorious release that was just a few pumps away. "Fuck me."

He gripped my hair and pulled my head back. He stopped deep inside me and I tightened around him, flexing and milking his cock. "What do you think I'm doing?" Miles nipped at my ear and throat. "You feel like paradise."

I writhed underneath him, squirming to feel the pounding drive of his body against mine again.

"Is this what you want?" he asked, and the bastard fucked me slowly. Too slowly.

A sob built up in my throat as I wiggled against him

desperately. "Please." I wasn't above begging, too greedy for the rush. "Make me come."

"With pleasure," he purred and picked up the pace.

I groaned in anticipation. I wanted him to pull my hair again. I wanted to be on top so I could grind and writhe on him again. I could hear the throbbing bass line of someone's music and my heart matched the beat. Miles's breathing was tortured, and the hard slap of our bodies drove me to that special place. I cried out, loud and long, and shook hard against him. My orgasm started in my toes and tingled all the way to the top of my head. He stiffened, shouted, and pulled my hips tight against him and I felt him empty himself into the condom.

We stayed like that, melted into each other, as our breathing got under control. Miles kissed my shoulder and eased out. I was a pile of goo on his desk. After a moment, he helped me upright and wrapped me in a soft blanket that smelled like his aftershave. Carrying me over to a wide leather couch opposite his desk, Miles sat down and settled me into his lap. Cuddling close, he kissed my forehead.

"I have a lead on Lisa," he said.

CHAPTER NINE

Miles Carvello

Jackie popped straight up in my arms. Her face was so close, I was distracted by her full lips. I wanted to kiss her again.

"Is she all right?"

"I don't know. It could be a dead end. It could lead to another clue." I didn't want her to get her hopes up.

"What's the lead?"

I told her about Paulie, Dee, and Zeke, leaving out the part about the drugs and pistol.

I liked that she was comfortable enough to stay in my arms and I was happy to keep hold of her. My job didn't afford a lot of downtime and I hadn't had sex in a few months. Now I was glad I'd waited. Jackie was special and one of a kind, even though her sister was pissing me off about how she was treating her family. Although, it *had* brought Jackie to my club. I was determined to make these few days I had with her into great memories that might lead her back to me the next time she could get away for a Vegas vacation.

"Do you think their disappearance has something to do with Lisa's?"

She shifted to sit down next to me. I was shitty with after-care, apparently. I wanted to make her feel that she mattered to me, that she wasn't just a horny fuck in my office. I wanted her to know I didn't do this with every new girl that worked in my club. But Jackie wasn't like the other girls. She focused on one thing with all her attention. A few minutes ago, it had been my cock. Now it was her sister. I was glad she wasn't clingy, but I had expected to cuddle for more than five seconds. I resisted the urge to kiss her so I could see the haze of lust take over her expression again. But we had all night. I could be romantic and take her out for dinner and drinks, before spending the rest of the evening seeing how many times I could make her come again. Once we tracked down Zeke and Lisa, Jackie was going to concentrate on having the time of her life. I would make sure of it.

"It seems too coincidental that the three of them disappeared right around the same time, but it's entirely possible that they're all unrelated instances."

"Let me get dressed and we can go." She hopped off the couch still wrapped in the blanket and headed to the door. But then she turned back. "Were you serious about firing me?"

"Yeah," I said.

"So I don't have to finish my set?"

"No."

"Do I still get to keep my tips?"

I chuckled. "Yeah, and Chance tipped you a hundred dollars." It had come over the headset as we walked back to my office.

"I didn't have sex in the VIP room," she said.

"Good." I didn't want to beat the shit out of Chance for something he had no clue about.

"I killed it tonight." She grinned at me.

Both on and off the stage. "I know," I said.

"Better than Lisa."

"I don't even remember Broadway's first dance."

Her face pinked up and I was entranced. Now, she blushed?

"So why did you fire me, then?" Jackie pouted and folded her arms over her chest.

I stood up and smiled when her eyes dropped to my half-mast cock. Yeah, I was ready for another go. But I had a feeling she would be distracted if we went for round two now. "I'm being selfish."

"How?" She frowned.

"I want you all to myself."

Blinking, she took a shaky breath. "I'd like that too."

"Are you okay with a vacation fling?"

"Obviously." She gestured to the couch. "But what if this lead of yours turns out to be nothing? Then I'm back to square one. Will you rehire me?"

"Do you really want to hustle men with your body?"

"I want to dance," she said.

"Not what I asked."

"No," she said reluctantly. "But if every night was like this one . . ."

"It wouldn't be."

"I know, but if that's the only way to see if that guy who was interested in Lisa comes back and to get the other dancers to trust me with what they know, I want to do it." She squared her shoulders and lifted her chin. "Is that going to be a problem?"

"Yeah," I said. "You're a distraction for me. A fantastic one, don't get me wrong. But I can't run my club with you on the stage. I'm not wired that way. If you're with me, then you're mine."

Jackie shivered and I started to reconsider round two. She could sit on my lap and grind on me to her heart's content. I took a step forward to lead her back to the couch.

"My sister has to be the priority," she said. But she was looking at my cock and licking her lips.

"Then, let's go see what we can find at Zeke's and Dee's homes. They could be dead ends or we could find out something worth pursuing. And then I want to take you out to a nice dinner, maybe a show."

She smiled and my heart stuttered. What the fuck was that all about? This was sex. Raw, hot, horny sex. When she smiled I should be thinking about her lips around my cock, not having my hormones flutter like I was a kid with his first crush.

"And then we're going back to your hotel room," I said, yanking her to me. Tossing the blanket aside, I slid my hand down the silky smooth skin of her belly. She parted her legs for me and I dipped just one finger inside her sticky wetness.

Gasping, Jackie clutched at my shoulders. I fingered her softly, aware that she might be a little sore after I took her so roughly. "And then, I'm going to explore every inch of you with my tongue." I murmured in her ear, nipping at her earlobe.

Reaching out, she trailed her fingernails up the shaft of my cock. "I've got plans of my own for you and it involves you flat on your back." She rubbed me just as slowly.

"Babe, why don't we go upstairs to my apartment? We can start the search tomorrow. Right now, I don't have the strength to let you go."

She eased away so my fingers fell out. She stroked me a few more times before letting me go. "No, I need a few hours to recover. I want some serious wall-banging sex later. After I give you the best damn blow job of your life."

Holy shit. I swallowed hard and couldn't move as she

wrapped the blanket around her like a toga. Jackie walked out of my office, tossing me a saucy wink over her shoulder.

She'd make me a fortune if I let her work prime hours. But she was leaving as soon as she found her sister, and for the first time in a long time I was feeling selfish enough to want something for myself.

I turned my Bluetooth back on and listened to the security chatter, hoping that would settle down my raging hardon. Nothing unusual was going on. I hadn't even been missed. Maybe I didn't have to work twenty-four seven in the bar. Jackie was a good way to ease into some kind of life-work balance. And then I remembered that my uncle's employees bailed on him before some assholes burned his place down with him in it. It had been three years since I got that terrible phone call from the Las Vegas police department and I thought about it every damn day since.

I couldn't afford to let myself be distracted and miss something important. My uncle had enemies and that animosity should have died with him, but I was more than prepared to take the fight to some of them out of revenge as well as self-preservation. The local gang was the Rivs and, after a rocky start when I first opened Dalton's two years ago, we'd come to a mutual agreement. However, I had to put about half of them in the hospital first. It almost came down to gunplay, but my reputation saved me. Leonidas, the leader of the Rivs, had a few Eurotrash cousins who owned some clubs I had worked at. Once I made a few phone calls, they told him to lay off Dalton's.

My entire life savings was sunk into this place and I had loyal employees who relied on me to provide them a paycheck and a safe place to work. I couldn't let them down. Taking the back entrance out of my office, I got into the elevator and keyed it for the top floor. After letting myself into my apartment above the club, I took a quick shower. I probably should have brought Jackie up here instead of fucking her on the couch in my office, but we would have never gotten out of bed. My cock still twitched from her touch and I would be hearing her eager screams in my head for a long time.

I threw on another pair of black jeans and a matching T-shirt. It was our club uniform, but it would be passable for a night on the town. Going back downstairs into the club area, I did a walk-through. It was getting busier and if it kept up, we were going to have a good night.

Chance was still missing and I could only hope he was enjoying himself with any other stripper than Jackie. Sienna gave me a nod as she gave one of the Aussie soccer players a lap dance. She had ten-dollar bills sticking out of her bra and thong. Say what you want about the Australians, they weren't afraid to tip the girls.

Later on, that might piss off the Americans who wanted the most bang for their buck. Little did they know it took a lot more than a few dollar bills to buy the kindness of the dancers. On stage Lavender was giving it her all to George Michael's "I Want Your Sex."

Highway raised an eyebrow when I walked up to him. He exaggerated an inhale.

"You smell pretty, sunshine. Want to fuck?"

"You're a charmer. I'm taking the night off. I'll see you tomorrow. Lock up and don't take any shit."

"This isn't like you." He looked over my head at some-thing. "But I can see why you're doing it."

Glancing over my shoulder, I saw a freshly scrubbed Jackie weaving through the crowd toward us. She wore a sundress with big purple flowers on it and sensible shoes. Her hair was back in a slick ponytail and she didn't look anything like La Vie Bohème in her street clothes. I wondered if she was back to wearing granny panties and her white cotton bra. I couldn't wait to find out.

"It's good to see you smile. You deserve some R&R," Highway said.

"I wasn't asking for permission," I retorted. "Besides I'm not completely off the clock. I want to make sure these disappearances aren't the harbinger of something more serious."

"You've got to stop using that word-a-day dictionary calendar. I don't know what those big words mean."

Like hell he didn't. Highway often pretended he was a dumb goon because it was easier.

"Give me a call if the shit hits the fan. I won't be too far away."

"I can manage it."

Jackie linked her arm through mine when she was close enough. She smiled up at me and I couldn't resist a kiss. Her leaving my office in a blanket and me leaving with her now was going to be all over the bar by tomorrow, but I didn't give a shit. I was staking a claim and sending a message. The dancers wouldn't think she was an outsider if they thought she was with me. They'd probably even suck up to her, hoping to get in my good graces. Ha, the joke was on them. I didn't have any. Or it could go the other way, if they thought she was getting special treatment because we were fucking. That's another reason I didn't want her dancing again.

I was determined to protect my bar and Jackie from people like Ginny and the criminals that killed my uncle. And unlike Uncle Johnny, I wasn't going to hope that the police would handle it. I planned to bring that shit right to the door of the motherfuckers who thought they could mess with what's mine.

CHAPTER TEN

Jackie Mitchell

Miles drove a Ford Mustang that had seen better days, but the muscle car suited him. I rolled the windows down and enjoyed the early evening sights on the Las Vegas strip. It was a dry heat because we were in the middle of the desert, but the breeze from the moving car made it worth it to forgo the AC so I could stick my head out the window and people watch. There was a part of me hoping to see Lisa in the crowd, even though I knew how delusional that was.

"Where are we going?"

"We're going to Zeke's house first. Highway said he hung out with your sister."

"Why didn't he tell me that yesterday? I could have talked to Zeke." I ran an exasperated hand through my hair.

Miles shrugged. "What's done is done."

It was because yesterday I had been an outsider. I had always been on the sidelines all my life. This was the first time that dancing made me fit in. I was going to miss the adventure of stripping, but I was glad not to have to spend time in the VIP room. It was much more enticing to think of spending time with Miles. Like later tonight. Digging my toes into my sandals, I replayed how he took me roughly from behind. I resisted the urge to lift my hips at the phantom cock I could still feel inside me.

"What are you thinking about?" Miles reached over to casually flip my skirt up my thighs.

Busted. I should be thinking about my sister. But I didn't want the naughty feelings born of freedom and decadence to go away. "I'm thinking about how much of your cock I can take down my throat."

Miles braked hard as we almost rear-ended the car in front of us. "You should come with a warning label."

I laughed and leaned my head on his shoulder. "I'll come any way you want."

"Yes, you will."

His voice made me shiver in all the right places. "I'm having fun."

"Good," he said. "Jeez, it's true what they say about the quiet types."

"You wouldn't even recognize me in New York." I stared out the windshield. "I would never strip in a New York club. Aside from being terrified I'd run into someone I know, I couldn't be this free so close to my responsibilities. The closest I've ever come was auditioning for a part in a show recently."

Reaching down, he linked his fingers through mine. "That's no way to go through life, sweetheart."

"I know. I'm trying to move beyond it. It's going slowly, but I'm getting there. This thing with Lisa set me back a few steps, but these past few days have made up for that."

"You're sexy and talented. You've been waiting in the wings too long."

I rubbed my cheek on his arm. "Will you pull my hair when I give you a blow job?"

"Jesus Christ," he said shakily. "Is that why you put it back into that ponytail?"

He reached over to give it a tug and I shamelessly moaned at him.

"Keep it up and I'll park and make you give me one before we go find Zeke."

Satisfied that I could keep a man like Miles Carvello on his toes, I eased back into my own seat. "No way. You promised me dinner and a show first."

He grunted. "Behave or the show you get to see will be in one of the seedier clubs with my cock inside you."

I blew out a shaky breath. I had a feeling if I said, "Yes, please," we'd be derailed from our quest. It was tempting, but if it turned out Lisa was at the place we were going to, then I could devote the rest of the week to making Miles Carvello my sex slave. Or me his. I was up for either.

He left the Strip and drove for a few miles. The city looked empty without all the bright lights and the bustle. "We're going into a rough neighborhood. Stay close and if things go down, run to the car and lock yourself in." He parked outside an apartment complex. After we got out of the Mustang, he locked it and tossed me the keys. "I mean it."

"I'm not a hero," I said. In fact, I was getting a little sleepy. I'd definitely have coffee with dinner. I didn't want to waste a moment doing something as mundane as sleeping.

"Good." He paused and took a deep breath. "I don't know what we're going to find. I don't know if Zeke is providing your sister room and board or if it's something more sinister. But no matter what happens, we're going to get her through this."

I nodded "Thanks."

Zeke's apartment building didn't have a security lock or, if it did, it wasn't working. Miles opened the door for me, but made me wait for him to go down the hallway first. Glancing down at his phone, he said, "Third floor. I don't trust that elevator. Let's take the stairs."

Padding up the metal staircase behind Miles, I resisted the urge to touch him. I wanted to lay my forehead on his wide back and let him be strong for me. My mind played havoc on my emotions as I pictured Lisa in trouble behind these closed doors. Angry voices spilled out into the hallways in several different languages. The smell of cooking cabbage and burnt bacon assaulted my nostrils.

Please let her be all right.

Miles stopped outside a door and stood to the side of the peephole. He banged on the door and waited. It flung open and a woman carrying a small child on her hip peeked out.

"What do you want?" she asked.

"I'm looking for Zeke."

A shadow of fear passed over her face. "He's not here."

"Where is he?"

"He went up to Pahrump."

"Why?" Miles drawled out.

"To chase a girl."

My breath caught in my throat. "Was it this girl?" I pushed by Miles to show the woman a picture of my sister.

"No," the woman said. "She was a blonde, somebody he worked with."

"Dee," Miles said quietly.

"Yeah, that's her. Look, my brother makes bad choices. He thinks with his little head." She set the toddler down. "Go play," she said to the child, who scampered inside. She stepped outside into the hallway with us and closed the door. "Does he owe you money?"

"No," Miles said. "I'm his boss from Dalton's."

Her eyes grew wide. "Are you hiring?"

"Yes," he said.

"I'm not like my brother. I'm always on time and I'm loyal to the job."

"What do you do?" he asked.

"I cook. I clean. I can do anything."

"Go see Liu at the club tomorrow. If he likes you, you're hired."

"Thank you," she said, making a quick sign of the cross. "I don't know if my brother is coming back. It depends on this woman. So you probably shouldn't hold his job for him."

"Do you know why Dee left for Pahrump?" Miles asked.

"Zeke said the girl had friends up there. He and she used to go up there a lot and stay the night. Then she decided to stay up there and not come back. Zeke got scared."

"Scared? Of what?" I asked.

"Of losing her." She looked over her shoulder at the closed door. "So he dropped everything and was determined to bring her back home to Vegas. Like I could fit another body in this apartment." She rolled her eyes.

"Did he say why she wanted to move to Pahrump?" I said.

"I think it's safer for her line of work up there."

"A cook?"

She looked at me like I was an idiot. "Yes, a cook."

I grabbed on to Miles's arm. He was steady and I needed that right now. "Was she being harassed at Dalton's?"

She snorted. "For all I know, Zeke was the one harassing her. She didn't ask him to come with her for a reason. But he didn't listen to me when I tried to tell him that." She stared up at Miles. "He liked working at your club. But it wasn't just the naked women. Zeke liked his coworkers in the kitchen too. He'd go out and party with them all the time. And he loves Las Vegas. I don't see him moving to Pahrump permanently. He's got too many friends here." She sighed. "But maybe it would be better if he stayed there. When he was younger, he would hang out on the streets all night and I worried myself to death. It's just us. Our parents are dead."

"When was the last time you heard from him?" I asked.

"This afternoon. He asked for money to put a deposit down on an apartment, but I think he was spinning me a line of bullshit." She shook her head. "I should get back in there before my kids tear the place apart. Thank you for the opportunity to interview at the club. I'm a hard worker."

"I can see that," Miles said.

"I could maybe take his job. I've been a waitress before. Although I'm not as young or as pretty as I used to be. Do you think that will be a problem?" She frowned.

"No," Miles said. "But if you feel uncomfortable, we have openings in the kitchen too."

"Thank you," she said again and turned to go.

"Wait," I said and thrust Lisa's picture at her again. "Have you ever seen this woman? Has your brother ever talked about Lisa or Broadway?"

"I'm sorry." The woman opened her door. "I haven't. She's not his type. You would be."

Craning my neck, I tried to look inside the apartment. I wasn't sure what I was expecting to see. Maybe Lisa tied up in the corner. But it looked like a normal apartment with a couple of kids racing around and the television blaring. "Me?"

"Yeah, a little trashy, but sweet."

I blinked down at my phone. Lisa didn't look trashy at all. She looked like a ballerina. "Trashy?" I ran a hand over my hair self-consciously. Then shook myself out of it. "Her name is Lisa. If Zeke calls, could you ask him if he's seen her?" I handed her one of my business cards. "And ask him to call me."

She looked at Miles and nodded. "Okay."

"We would really appreciate it," he said.

She gave him a tentative smile and slipped back inside her apartment. We walked back down to the car.

"I think she meant trashy as a compliment," Miles said.

"Does she look trashy?" I shoved the picture at Miles.

"No. She looks like she has a stick up her ass."

"Would you have fucked her in your office?"

"I didn't."

"But if you and she had chemistry in the audition, like you and I did—"

"We didn't. Hell, Jackie, I barely remember her. And what I do remember is she was a difficult employee, a snob, and everyone thought she was a bitch."

"Everyone but that guy who kept coming back for her. Do you keep security tapes?" That should have been the first question out of my mouth when I met him, but he had set me so off kilter that I still wasn't thinking straight.

"Only for the week and then we write over them."

"Why? You should keep them in the cloud forever. In case of things like this."

Miles frowned as he considered it. I tossed him the keys and we got inside the car.

"You might be right."

"Well, that doesn't help me now," I said, trying not to be too dejected. "What's in Pahrump and how long a drive is it?"

Miles squinted at the traffic and for a moment I didn't think he was going to answer me. "It's about an hour and a half. And they've got casinos and wineries."

"Any of those places offer room and board?"

He cleared his throat. "We don't even know if Lisa is with Zeke or Dee."

"It looks like they're the last people to have seen her." I nibbled on my fingernail. "I don't want to be running all over Nevada on a wild goose chase, though. But if Dee was scared off, it's possible it was the same thing that scared Lisa off."

"If that's the case, I want to know who or what is threatening my employees," Miles said.

"Unless you have an address in Pahrump for Dee, we're stuck until Zeke calls his sister. If she even gives him the message."

"She'll give him the message. She wants a job at Dalton's. She's going to do whatever she can to get in the door."

Miles sounded confident, so I chose to believe him. Pulling down the visor, I looked in the mirror. "Do you think I look trashy?"

"In a good way."

The way he smiled made that the biggest compliment of my life.

"And you're so very sweet, just like she said," he continued. "I can't wait to taste you again."

My nipples tightened against my bra. I wanted to fling the damn thing off. I knew I should have just worn the pasties. "Where do you want to go to dinner?" I asked. "My hotel does room service."

Miles started the car. "What hotel are you staying at?"

"The Wynn."

He pulled out into traffic and my heart fluttered. I was going to get laid again. I squirmed in my seat. Best. Vacation. Ever.

And then my phone rang.

I gasped and fumbled for my purse. "Oh no," I said, looking at who was calling.

"Is it Lisa?"

"Worse. It's my mother." I wanted to chuck the phone out the window. "I've got to take this, otherwise she's going to be a real nuisance."

"Go ahead."

Closing my eyes, I tried to center myself. The ringing stopped.

"Looks like she gave up," Miles said.

"Wait for it," I muttered, and like clockwork the phone went off again. "Yes, Mom," I said, answering it on the second ring. I thought I'd kept the aggravation out of my voice.

"How's your sister?"

I debated how much to tell her. "I still haven't found her."

"Why not?"

"She's not answering her cell and she moved out of her apartment about three weeks ago. She also quit her job around that time."

"Well, where is she?"

"That's what I'm trying to find out. I'm asking her friends and the people she worked with."

"She's probably auditioning for a production down there. You should hit all the talent scouts. Maybe you're being replaced."

She did *not* just say that.

My mother continued on, oblivious that she'd fired an arrow into my gut. "Get a newspaper and find out who's hiring for a lead dancer."

"No one uses paper anymore." That was the most scathing thing I could come up with.

"I'm sure now that she's no longer bartending . . ."

Stripping, I corrected mentally.

"It's only a matter of time before she calls in to tell us that she's booked a new gig. Really, Jackie, you should have hustled more for your sister."

"Give me the phone," Miles said, reaching for it.

No, I mouthed at him and scooted away so he couldn't take it from me. "Well, I'm glad you're not worried. I guess I'll go back to New York."

"Don't you dare."

"I'm sorry, I'm going to dare to do whatever I want." That wasn't much better, but at least this time my attitude got through to her and her tone switched from strident to cajoling.

"Jackie, your sister isn't good with contracts or numbers. She needs you to stop people from taking advantage of her. Find her before she signs away all of her rights. Lisa is an artist. All she wants to do is dance. She doesn't care about the mundane things like we do."

"I'm losing cell service," I lied. "Gotta go. I'll call you when I hear something." I hung up. I wanted to turn it off, but I didn't dare in case Lisa or someone who knew where she was called. I stared at it with trepidation. A few minutes clicked past, but Mom didn't call back. Sighing, I tossed the phone back into my purse.

"If you don't mind me saying so, your mom's a bitch."

"And if I do mind?" I didn't, and it actually felt good to have someone take my side against my mother instead of trying to explain her behavior away.

"Then I'm sorry to be the one to tell you, but your mom's a bitch."

"Third time is the charm."

"She's a fucking bitch."

"Thanks for that." I wrapped my arms around his and laid my head against his shoulder.

"I'm sensing the room service mood has been broken," Miles said.

"A little bit, yeah."

"Dee lived with her mother. If you're not all mothered out, we could try there and see if we get lucky before getting lucky."

I kissed his arm because that coaxed a small smile out of me. "That sounds like a good idea."

"Has she always been like this?"

I nodded. "Sometimes she's worse. Usually I can ignore her. I've had to grow a thick skin when it comes to her blatant favoritism of Lisa. Sometimes though," I said. "She still makes me feel like crying."

"If she was in my club, I'd toss her out on her ass."

"I think I'd pay money to see that."

"Why does she favor Lisa?"

"My therapist thinks she's living vicariously through my sister. Mom's always been in love with the theater, but she didn't have the talent. Lisa was a prodigy and I was merely good. We didn't have a lot of money, so it made sense to her to promote Lisa."

"While you got left holding the bag?"

"Lisa's bags, yes. And later her calendar and her bookings."

"Why did you do it?"

"Well, at first I had no choice. But after I moved out, I guess it was just habit. And the job pays well. It was numbingly boring and gut wrenching to make her dreams come true. I compartmentalized a lot of it."

"You locked yourself away from your life?"

I wrinkled my nose. "You make it sound so dramatic, but yeah, in a way. I guess that's why it feels so good to be so trashy in Las Vegas."

"You're one of the best dancers I've ever seen."

Blinking back tears, I clutched his arm tighter. "I needed to hear that."

"You know, maybe you should see if there are any shows hiring."

"You think Lisa's auditioning to be a showgirl?"

He snorted. "If she is, she won't last past her first audition. She couldn't do four sets of three minutes every hour without having to ice her knee."

"Then what would I find out at a cattle call?"

"You could find out that your mother doesn't know shit

about talent and that you could become a Las Vegas showgirl."

I giggled nervously. He had to be joking. I looked up at his face. He was completely serious. "But I can't get time off from my job in New York to work as a showgirl."

"So don't take the job."

Don't take the job? Was he nuts? I had wanted to be a Rockette from the very first Christmas I saw them dance at Rockefeller Center. A Vegas showgirl complete with feathered harness and the glittery body suits was the epitome of professional dancer to me.

"How much do they make?"

"About 40K a year, I think."

I couldn't live on that in Manhattan, but maybe I could in Las Vegas. Wait, what was I even thinking? I had a life in New York, a great career, and my family was there. My phone buzzed and I dug it out to look at it. Winter storm warning was in effect in Manhattan for the next forty-eight hours. Letting go of Miles, I rolled my window down and let the hot desert air buffet my face.

A Las Vegas showgirl.

Me.

"Do you think I can do it?"

"Yes."

"How? We've only known each other a few days."

"I've seen you dance. You're gorgeous. You have great legs." Miles ticked off the list on his fingers. "You're not afraid of anything."

I gave a short laugh. I was afraid of everything.

"You're a free spirit."

"Me?"

"Who else would decide to become a stripper to find her sister? And did I mention, you're the best dancer I've ever seen. And I've seen a lot of them. Granted, most of them were naked," he admitted. "But you outshone them all. If I didn't want you for myself, you'd be making thirty thousand a month in my club until someone stole you away from me."

This time I did laugh. "Only if all my VIP clients were you and Chance."

Miles scowled. "Forget about Chance."

"He's going to help us find Lisa." I recounted the conversation Chance and I had.

"It's really tough to hate him," he said. "He's a nice bloke."

"Then don't. You've got nothing to be jealous about. I want you, not him."

"Good." Miles gave me a cocky smile and I was in the mood again.

Too bad we had arrived at Dee's mother's place.

We were in a more upscale part of town than before. I knew this because the communities were gated and the security at the kiosk outside of Dee's mother's condo was eyeballing Miles's tattoos.

"Who are you here to see?"

Miles looked at his sticky note. "Eleanor Brandon."

"One moment."

"If she tells us to fuck off, let's go to the Wynn," I said in Miles's ear while fondling him through his jeans when the guard was busy calling to see if we were welcome or not.

"You got it." He thumbed my nipple and it made me gasp.

Unfortunately, the guard waved us through and told us where to park. Inside the gates, we could be in any city in the world. The shrubs and bushes were green and healthy, even though we were in the desert. As we walked up to the condo, a stunning woman in her mid-fifties stormed out of the house wearing a white one-piece bathing suit and a turban. The gauzy coverup she was hastily pulling on floated behind her like a cape.

"Eleanor Brandon?" I asked.

The woman nodded and turned to Miles. "Are you Miles Carvello?"

"Yes," he said.

"Because of you, my daughter is a whore."

And then she slapped Miles hard across the face.

CHAPTER ELEVEN

Miles Carvello

I took the crack even though I could have easily avoided it. It stung, but I sold it by rocking my head to the side. If it made Dee's mother feel good, and calm enough to explain the bullshit she was spewing, it would be worth it.

"She was going to be a chef. She was going to Cordon Bleu. Did you know that? Do you even care?"

"She was a shitty cook." At least that's what Liu always said. "Lazy in the kitchen and her knife skills just plain sucked."

Yeah, that wasn't the right thing to say. So much for calming her down. Before she could swing again, Jackie stepped in. I squared off on the mother and she blinked at me, probably noticing that I could break her in half and stuff her in the dumpster. Not that I would, but she didn't have to know that.

"I think there's been a misunderstanding," Jackie said soothingly.

"No, there hasn't." Eleanor's eyes filled with tears. "She's a hooker at the Moondust Cherry Ranch."

"In Pahrump?" Jackie whispered.

"Yes." Eleanor started to cry.

I hated when chicks did that. Jackie found some tissues in that gargantuan purse she carried and handed her some.

"Thank you."

"My name is Jackie Mitchell. Miles is helping me look for my sister, Lisa, and I think . . ." Jackie took a shaky breath. "I think Lisa might be with Dee. Can we go inside and talk?"

Eleanor glared at me. "He led them to do it. It's that damn club. I knew I should have forbidden her to work there."

"No." Jackie shook her head. "Miles is trying to find them. He cares about all his employees. When he found out Dee went missing, he went to Zeke's place to track her down."

"That boy." Dee's mother shook her head. "He's trouble. If Miles didn't convince her she could make more money selling her body, then Zeke did." She scrubbed at her tears angrily. "You might as well come in."

I nodded brusquely, but Jackie jammed an elbow into my side. "I wish we were meeting under different circumstances," I said, absently rubbing my ribs.

Eleanor really looked at me this time and I could tell she liked what she saw. Well, maybe that would help open her up to our questions. I didn't feel like smiling at her, but it seemed she didn't need it. Straightening her shoulders, she let the gauzy wrap flutter down her back and put a sway in her step as she led us inside her condo.

"Behave," Jackie whispered fiercely to me.

I kissed Jackie quick because I wanted to, and she gaped at me. She was still blushing when Eleanor led us to what she called the sunroom and bade us to sit on uncomfortable steel chairs that had been polished like chrome on a Harley. "Can I get you something to eat or drink?" Eleanor rang a little bell and an honest-to-God manservant appeared out of nowhere. He was dressed in a formal suit and jacket with tails. In this heat?

"We're good," I said.

"Nonsense, let me get you a drink. It's the least I can do after behaving so horribly." Eleanor leaned a little to give me a flash of cleavage, but I didn't drop my eyes. Tits were a dime a dozen in my line of work and the only ones I wanted were Jackie's.

"I'll have a beer," I said to the manservant.

"Oh you must try the lemon shandy."

I winced. "Yeah, no. Fruit doesn't belong in beer."

I got elbowed again.

"That sounds very refreshing," Jackie said.

I made eye contact with the manservant and he gave me a small nod and left the room.

"This is my sister, Lisa." Jackie pulled out that damn photo and went into the whole spiel.

Letting my mind wander, I looked around the condo. It was an expensive setup. I didn't go much for high fashion, but the place had character. There was marble and stainless steel everywhere, but one whole wall was a window that looked out over the desert and Lake Las Vegas. The manservant in his ridiculous little outfit was back with the drinks almost immediately. I took a sip of my beer. It was lemon free and surprisingly good.

"You must be terribly worried," Eleanor said, putting a comforting hand over Jackie's.

"Did Dee ever mention Lisa or Broadway? That was the name Lisa danced under."

Eleanor snatched her hand back. "Your sister was a stripper?"

She said *stripper* the same way she'd said *hooker*. I didn't like how ashamed Jackie looked. "My girls dance, nothing else," I said. "Your daughter stayed in the kitchen. She got paid a decent wage, but the dancers make double her salary. Dee wasn't talented enough to be a dancer, perhaps that's why—"

Jackie kicked me under the table, and I amended what I was going to say.

"Perhaps she saw a faster way to pay for her Cordon Bleu tuition."

"You could have paid her better," Eleanor said, looking down her nose at me.

"You could have paid her tuition." I circled my beer around, indicating the house.

Eleanor deflated. "I should have. But she's always been so unfocused. I thought if I made her earn her tuition, she would appreciate it more. I never thought she would sell her body, though." She gave a bitter laugh. "After all I've done to give her the life I never had."

"Are you sure that's what she's doing?" Jackie said. "Maybe she just told you that to make you feel guilty or upset enough so that you would offer to pay the tuition."

I hid a snort. "Denial ain't just a river in Egypt," I muttered and moved away before I could get another kick. I got beat up less at Dalton's on frat night.

Eleanor grabbed onto that like it was a lifeline. "You think so?"

"I don't know," Jackie said. "I'm just looking for my sister. Did Dee ever mention her?"

"No. She didn't talk about work a lot. She hated her boss." Eleanor flicked me a look. "Not you, the chef."

"Is that why you told him you haven't seen her in two days?"

Eleanor made a face. "I wasn't about to tell him that she quit to become a hooker. I still have hope that I can talk her out of this mess and get her back into the kitchen. I just doubt it will be yours after what he put her through."

"Liu can be a diva," I admitted. He also didn't suffer fools and ruled the kitchen like a medieval fiefdom. Dee wasn't completely incompetent, but she didn't move as fast as Liu liked. I hadn't thought there was that much friction between the two, but maybe I didn't see it because I didn't want to. "Dee should have come to me if there was a problem," I grumbled, mostly because I was feeling guilty.

"She didn't hate her job and, aside from Liu, she liked the people she worked with. They would go out and party after work. I'd catch her coming in at all hours of the morning. It's possible that she knew your sister." Eleanor took a long pull of her lemon shandy and slipped the gauzy coverup completely off so she sat there in her bathing suit. It was obvious now that it wasn't her first drink of the day as she tried to catch my eye. "I hope she didn't lead Lisa down this path."

"You said she didn't talk about work, but you recognized the name of one of my waiters, Zeke. What's the story with him?" I asked.

"She went out with him a few times. I didn't like him, but she seemed to have a good time with him. He called the house if she didn't pick up her phone." Eleanor rolled her eyes. "I had to have a good talking to him about boundaries and he wised up after that."

"Did Dee ever mention someone threatening her at work?" Jackie asked.

Eleanor frowned. "Not that she told me, but there are bad elements that hang around clubs like yours."

I clenched my jaw. "Not my bar."

She shrugged with one shoulder and patted her turban delicately. "I'm familiar with the area."

"Not lately."

Jackie missed with her kick this time too. I was going to spank her ass red if she didn't stop it. I tried to put that into a glare, but she wasn't looking at me.

"Would you ask her about that the next time she calls?" Jackie asked. "And ask if she's seen Lisa?"

"I'll call her right now," Eleanor said and pulled the latest iPhone out of the pocket of her coverup. It had sparkles and glitter all over it. I had to look away before I was blinded. "Hello, darling," she said into the phone after a moment. "Your boss, Miles, came to see me. He's offering to hire you back at double your salary."

I choked on my beer. What the fuck?

"I'm sure something could be done about Liu."

There was a long pause while Eleanor listened. At least Dee was answering her mother's calls, which was more than I could say for Lisa.

"I didn't raise you like this, Deidre Marie Jones."

Jackie raised her eyebrows at me. "She got the full name treatment. That's how you know it's serious."

I kicked her in the shin.

"Ow," she said, rubbing it.

"How do you like it?"

She stuck her tongue out at me.

"Keep it up," I warned her in a low voice.

"I don't care how much you make a night!" Eleanor shrieked, banging her palm on the table so hard the glasses jumped. "I don't want to know anything about it. I just want you to come home. I'll pay for Cordon Bleu. You won't have to go back to that nasty bar."

"Hey," I said warningly.

"Dalton's is a really nice place," Jackie said.

I gawked at her in surprise. I hadn't expected her to defend my club.

Eleanor listened intently to what her daughter was saying and then she gave a huge sigh. "You need to leave."

"Ask her about Lisa," Jackie hissed.

"Right." Eleanor closed her eyes and rubbed her forehead. "Have you seen any of your coworkers while you've been there? Zeke or Lisa?"

"She might know her as Broadway," Jackie reminded her.

"Lisa or a Broadway. You have?" Eleanor nodded at Jackie. Jackie clutched my arm. "Is she okay?"

"Is she all right?" Eleanor repeated into the phone. She listened for a minute and then nodded at Jackie.

Jackie bit back a sob and then threw herself into my arms. I had to stand up, otherwise the chair would have dumped us on the floor. "She's all right," Jackie repeated and squeezed me tight. "I'm going to kill her." Jackie thrust herself away from me. "Can I speak to her?" she said to Eleanor with a mock sweetness.

I'm not sure what Eleanor saw on her face, but she recoiled back from it. "Is she with you?" she asked her daughter.

Eleanor shook her head. "She's not there."

"Can I speak to *Dee?*" Jackie emphasized.

Eleanor cleared her throat. "Darling, Lisa's sister is here and she's very worried about her. Would you like to talk with her?" After a moment, Eleanor handed the phone to Jackie.

"Hi, my name is—" Jackie didn't get to finish her sentence. She tensed and then her knees wobbled. I quickly came up behind her and wrapped my arms around her. She was shaking. "Okay. Okay. I will. Thank you."

She handed the phone back to Eleanor. Turning in my arms, she looked at me and shook her head. "We've got to go."

"You got it." I was more than ready to get out of here.

"When can you come home?" Eleanor asked her daughter.

"Let's go." Jackie tugged on my arm and made for the door.

"Eleanor, it's been real," I said. "Dee is not going to be rehired. She can work at Denny's for all I care."

"I think that's for the best," Eleanor said, looking up from her conversation to sneer at me.

When we were back in the car, Jackie let out a small scream of rage.

"What's going on?"

"Lisa was bartending at the Moondust Cherry Ranch two weeks ago."

"They give room and board?"

"I doubt it. Not unless she was doing things other than bartending. Anyway, she's no longer there. We're still two weeks behind her. Dee wants to talk with me tomorrow, though."

"Why not tonight? We're only a couple of hours away." I gripped the steering wheel. I was up for a drive.

"She's got a full plate tonight. She's not quitting her job and coming home. She didn't want to tell her mother that."

"She's an adult."

"So's Lisa, but at least Dee answers the phone when her mother calls. I'm not telling my mother that Lisa decided to become a hooker."

"We don't know that she did."

"No," Jackie sighed. "We don't, but why else would Dee want to talk to me in person unless it was to tell me something awful?"

"Lisa could have gotten another bartending gig."

"Or maybe she decided to become a personal escort for the mysterious guy." Jackie groaned. "I'm not sure I even want to know anymore. I just want her to call our mother. I'm still going to drive out there first thing." She turned to me. "You're coming with me, right?"

I wanted to, but I had to meet with Grier in the morning. "I can't do it first thing. Can we go after lunch?"

"You don't have to go with me," she said, with a disappointed smile.

"Yes, I do. Please wait for me."

"Are there a lot of whorehouses in Pahrump?"

I hesitated. "Yeah."

"And you knew that when Zeke's sister mentioned where Zeke was going?"

I could sense the danger in the air. She was pissed and wanted to take out her anger on someone. I turned on the car.

"Answer me, Miles."

Squinting through the windshield, I looked around for security cameras. It didn't look like the gated community had any in the inner parking lots. Good. I drove deeper into the complex and pulled into what was probably a resident's parking spot. I wasn't planning on being here long. I turned off the car.

"Miles," Jackie said in a louder voice. "Did you know—?"

I wrapped my hand around her ponytail and pulled her head close to mine, cutting off her sentence with a hard kiss. Thrusting my tongue into her mouth, I pushed my hand up her shirt. Cotton bra. I smiled against her lips. She struggled for about half a second and then she tugged up my T-shirt.

Jackie traced her nails over my chest, digging in slightly against my abs. Pulling her head back by her ponytail, I sank my teeth lightly against her throat and she whimpered.

Kissing up to her ear, I growled. "I suspected. I didn't want you to be upset if it turned out to be nothing."

"I'm sorry," she whispered. "I'm not mad at you."

"Wait for me tomorrow before going up to see Dee?"

"I haven't decided." She smirked.

I kissed her again, sliding my lips over hers. I was deliberately rough, and she ground her mouth just as hard against mine. I pulled her hair again and she panted out a whimper. The sound went straight to my cock.

"Are you going to wait for me?" I asked again, pulling her ponytail to tilt her head back.

"You're starting to convince me," she said, her eyes glazed over with passion.

"I guess I'll have to try harder." I went back to her mouth because she was irresistible.

Jackie fumbled with the button and zipper on my pants.

I reached up under her skirt and got a handful of granny panties. I chuckled. Jackie groped inside my underwear and pulled out my cock. "You want something?" I said, my voice husky. I leaned my head back on the headrest and enjoyed her firm strokes.

"Don't forget to pull my hair."

My eyes went wide as she leaned over and engulfed me deep in her throat. My fingers tightened on her ponytail and she moaned around my cock. The vibration nearly sent me into orbit. I let her slide her mouth up and down, watching her lovingly suck and lick me. She looked up at me with laughter in her eyes and took me deep before sliding me all the way out of her mouth. She made a popping sound as the tip came free. Her lips were puffy from my kisses.

"Was that all right?" she asked, batting her eyelashes at me.

I pulled her hair and guided her head back down. "I didn't say stop."

Her entire body shivered, and she gave a little scream when I bucked my hips up. The scream turned into a moan when I held her head there and fucked her mouth with small soft strokes. I lifted her up by the ponytail, still wrapped around my fist, and brought her up so I could kiss her sweetly, as she took in deep gulps of air.

"I'm going to have to switch hands," I said, untwisting her hair from my fingers.

"Why is that?" she purred, kissing me.

I pushed her back down toward my lap. She eagerly took me in her mouth again and bobbed her head up and down with slick slurping sounds that had my eyes rolling back so hard in my head I saw stars. I flipped up her skirt. Her white granny panties were in my way, but I would do my best. Reaching between her legs, I pushed away the soaking wet fabric between her legs and rubbed my fingers through her soft folds.

Jackie bobbed her head faster. Each slide of her mouth drew another ragged breath from me. I fingered her, trying hard to find that little button from this angle. I wasn't quite making it, so I thrust three fingers inside her as deep as I could. Her thighs locked around my wrist as she rocked back against them. I used my free hand to tug up on her ponytail.

"I'm going to fucking explode." I tried to pull her up, but she swallowed around me instead.

"Oh fuck," I moaned.

She writhed on my fingers, but never stopped licking and sucking.

I started to shake. My entire body clenched. She was dragging everything out of me, and I was powerless to stop her. I desperately wanted her to come, but I lost all control of everything when she swallowed again. I was deep in the back of her mouth and I couldn't stop the floodgates as her body moved in time with my thrusting hips. I pulled her hair as I came, pumping into her as the world ignited into fiery pulses of pleasure.

"Fuck. Fuck. Fuck!" I chanted. It was the only word I knew. When she pulled away from me, I was completely boneless and entirely under her spell.

"Did you?" I asked.

She licked some of my come off her lip and shook her head. "Nope. You owe me."

I reached for her, but she slid back into the passenger seat.

"You're good for it."

I stared at her open-mouthed, still unable to process anything but the feeling of her wet mouth taking everything I could give her.

"Do you want me to drive?" she asked sweetly.

Yeah, I was definitely paddling that ass red later.

CHAPTER TWELVE

Jackie Mitchell

"How was that for trashy?" I asked Miles once he recovered enough to operate the motor vehicle.

"Five stars," he rasped.

My body still hummed from the rush of enjoying his body. I almost wanted to play with myself while he watched, but I was genuinely afraid he was going to crack up the car.

"I still want dinner and a show."

"Anything you want."

I was having a hard time managing my emotions. On the one hand, I was giddy and horny and loving every minute of being with Miles. That was Las Vegas Jackie. New York Jackie was a strung-out mess of worry, anger, and frustration. It was no wonder that I liked Las Vegas Jackie better. She was a hell of a good time.

But I had to get Las Vegas Jackie under control so we could find Lisa once and for all and then Las Vegas Jackie could have the rest of the week and Miles all to herself. Miles's phone rang.

"Is that *your* mother this time?" I asked, feeling restless. Maybe we could stop back at my hotel for a quickie before dinner.

"Not likely," he said, flicking a glance down to his phone. "Shit."

"What?"

"It's Highway." Miles brought the phone up to his ear. "What? Are you busting my balls? This better not be a fucking joke. All right. I'll be there as soon as I drop Jackie off."

My heart sank. "What's the matter?"

"Apparently there's a gas leak in the club."

"Oh no."

"I don't fucking buy it, but they had to clear out the bar and I'm hemorrhaging money until I can get there and yell at the inspectors for shutting me down." He tossed the phone into the middle console with disgust. "I'm sorry. I know I promised you a night out."

"That's okay," I said. "Take me back to the Wynn. I'll order some room service and we can rent a movie when you're done with this mess."

He quirked an eyebrow at me. "Are you sure?"

"Well, I suppose we could watch porn, but I got to be honest, I get bored and want to fast forward to the good parts."

"You're perfect, you know?" He stroked his thumb down my cheek.

"Far from it, and I might jump you before you get time to eat so maybe have a sandwich before you come over."

"I've got to keep my strength up."

I was disappointed, but I'd live. To be honest, I was pretty tired. I had hit the ground running—dancing—ever since I landed. It wouldn't kill me to take it easy tonight. Miles pulled right up to the cul-de-sac entrance to the hotel and kept the doors locked while I kissed him goodbye. I could certainly get used to having him in my bed for the rest of my time here. When I was sure he was as hot and bothered as me, I shifted back to my own seat. He unlocked the door and the doorman held it open for me.

"1492," I said as I exited the car.

"The year Columbus discovered America?"

"My room number." I let myself look my fill of him, uncaring that we were holding up people who wanted to get into the hotel. I wanted to take a picture of him. My lover. Just to prove to myself when he was gone that I didn't dream him up.

"I'll see you later," he said.

I floated up to the room, remembering the feel of Miles against me. I felt like dancing, but honestly, my feet were killing me. When I got up to my room, I ran a hot bath. Dumping a whole container of the complimentary sweet bath salts into the tub, I shucked off my clothes and put on the fluffy white robe and slippers they provided. Bliss. I flipped through the room service menu trying to find something that would keep for a couple of hours if Miles was delayed. I wound up picking two club sandwiches and subbed the fries for pasta salad.

After I placed the order, I put on the television music channel. The bath was calling my name. The quick shower I had taken at Dalton's was just to clean up instead of soaking into my overworked muscles, so the bath was going to feel decadent. The smell of lavender was making my eyelids heavy. I had to hold it together at least until room service got here. I might as well check my e-mail, so I didn't get avalanched next week.

I didn't want to think of Lisa, but she crept into my thoughts anyway. I was debating whether to let her know I was hot on her trail, but I didn't want to spook her into hiding. Three weeks ago, she met a gray haired man, quit her job and moved out of her apartment in Las Vegas. Two weeks ago, she was working in a brothel slinging drinks after an unsuccessful run at trying to be a dancer. Was she living with him or did he convince her that she could dance horizontally instead? I stopped clicking through my e-mails when I realized I wasn't comprehending a word of what I was reading. I called Lisa on the off chance that she would pick up. She didn't. I wanted to tell her I knew she worked at the brothel, but again, I didn't want to scare her off.

"Stop being a selfish bitch and call me."

I probably shouldn't have said that, but I was pretty damn mad at her.

Staring at my phone, I wanted to call Miles, but I didn't want to come off as needy. Just because I was on vacation, I shouldn't expect him to drop his responsibilities. And yet, it felt so damn good to be the center of attention and number one in someone's life—even if it were for just one day.

It had been a pretty good day. I got to dance. I made some cash. I got laid. I blew a guy in his muscle car. And if I were lucky, I'd get the chance to roll around on the mattress with him this time.

I called him. The animal attraction was dialed up to holy shit between the two of us, but I wanted to get to know him. I knew that was stupid. I was leaving in a few days. You didn't date a vacation fling, you took all the good stuff and left out all the drama.

I got his voice mail too.

"1492. Knock hard if I don't answer, I'm getting sleepy. But I still want you."

That sounded trashy and sweet.

Scrolling through pictures of him on the Internet, I couldn't believe this tough guy was all mine.

"For the week," I reminded myself and stretched myself out in the hot water.

Bathtubs were the best for fantasies. While I lay there soaking, I let myself dream that I'd auditioned for a Las Vegas show. Like my off-Broadway deal, I would be content to start small in the chorus and work my way up to lead dancer. I kicked up a few times, splashing water everywhere. Wincing, I shifted position. I was still a little sore from my time at Dalton's and then being wildly fucked in Miles's office.

I wondered what he was doing now and if he was thinking of me. I wish he had picked up.

Shaking my head, I went back to my fantasy. I'd be a Las Vegas showgirl and Miles would be my boyfriend—a boyfriend who was surrounded every night with beautiful, naked women. Groaning, I sank under the water. I'd be eaten alive with jealousy within the first week.

In fact, what if Miles had already handled the gas leak and was back in the club right now? Would he choose to stay there tonight to make sure everything was all right instead of coming over? And if he did, would I have the right to be pissed? I flicked the water in agitation. Now I was making up things to get mad at. As if I didn't have enough rage building up for Lisa and her perhaps pimp.

A quick text never hurt, right?

How are things? Are you almost done? When are you coming over? I'm horny.

No. Just no. I deleted the text.

I wanted to talk to someone. My mother was out. Miles was busy. I didn't know anyone else here. And then I remembered Chance. I bet he could help me out. I called him up and he answered immediately.

"Jackie, my favorite stripper." *Strip-pah.*

His accent was the bomb. I heard a low background noise of people talking and dishes rattling. It didn't sound like he was in a club.

"Were you guys still at Dalton's when the gas leak got called in?"

"Yeah, too bad too. Things were starting to get good."

"Did you smell anything?" I stared at my toes, which were getting all wrinkly in the tub. I should probably schedule a pedicure. I wouldn't even expense it to Lisa if she called Mom this week.

"Nah, but my senses were a little dulled by all that tequila."

"Where are you guys now?"

"We're grabbing something to eat and trying to decide if we want to gamble or go looking for trouble."

"Are you guys up for a road trip?"

"What have you got in mind?"

"Lisa was spotted at the Moondust Cherry Ranch in Pahrump. That's about two hours from here."

"Cherry Ranch, huh?"

"Chicken Ranch," I said.

"That's a big step from stripper."

"She was bartending two weeks ago there, but I'm worried she might have expanded her job search to the other ranches and other occupations. Do you think your friends could go to the neighboring . . . um . . . brothels and look for Lisa?"

Chance laughed for a good half a minute. "Let me get this straight, luv. You want me to convince this bunch to go look around a house of ill repute."

I winced. "Several of them, actually. You know prostitution is legal there, right?"

"I am aware," he said solemnly. "Okay, let me see if I can tear these louts from their burgers. Oi, you want to go to a crib and check out some Mollies?"

"Bonzer!" seemed to be the response.

"I don't know, Jackie luv. They seem to want to go out in the desert and watch some bush telly."

"I'm not sure I even want to know what that means," I said.

"It means if your sister is out there, I'll find her."

"Thanks, Chance."

There was a knock on my door.

"I've got to go. If you find out anything call me. Doesn't matter what time."

"You got it."

Sloshing out of the tub, I wrapped the robe around myself. I hoped it was Miles, but it was room service. I should have gotten the fries, I thought. At least for myself. I signed the receipt, tipping well. I was feeling hopeful and wanted to pass along the good karma vibes. After the delivery person left, I devoured half the sandwich before remembering it was late at night and I should probably take it easy. But I was so hungry I wound up eating both sandwiches.

"I warned him," I said as I took both bowls of pasta salad and sat in the enormous king-size bed. I turned on the television and binge-watched reruns of *The Big Bang Theory* until I fell asleep.

———

Miles Carvello

"At least it's not raining," Highway grumbled.

I couldn't even speak I was so angry. It was bad enough they evacuated my bar, but they also locked it down until the gas company sent someone out. It was hurry up and wait, so I sent the staff home, promising to pay them for the wasted night. Highway had decided to stay because he apparently thought I wanted the company.

I didn't.

We were told to stand as far away from the building as possible. I went across the street and paced up and down in front of the pawn shop until the owner shooed me away. I settled for leaning against the bail bondsman's wall and glared at the gas truck and the workers milling around trying to get a reading. They weren't going to get one because there wasn't a damn leak.

"This is bullshit. If we were on the Strip, we'd be back up again in the hour."

Liu would have noticed if there had been a gas leak. Certainly, Highway would have. No, this had been an anonymous tip that was credible enough that the city cut the gas for the entire block and sent out an ambulance and a couple of squad cars until the gas company got there. Seeing the area cordoned off made me want to rip down and shred the tape. It reminded me of what Uncle Johnny's club had looked like after the fire.

"Somebody's fucking with us. I bet it's those twat frat boys. I bet someone's daddy is in on it."

I grunted. It was possible.

"Did you pay protection to the Rivs?" Highway asked quietly.

That stopped me in my tracks. "No. They tried the gang shit with me two years ago. I told them to fuck off then and when they tried to make it ugly, I made it costly for them to continue on with the protection racket on my club. Leonidas and I have an understanding."

Leonidas had a gang of thugs with their fingers in all sorts of nasty areas. Lucky for me, drugs paid off better than protection rackets.

Highway sniffed. "Then maybe it was these assholes"—he

jerked his thumb in the direction of the pawn shop and the bail bondsman—"that called in the fake gas leak. They're shelling out fifteen percent a week. Maybe they don't like that you're not."

The pawn shop was owned by two German brothers who hated both Uncle Johnny's club and, most recently, my club. They thought we cost them customers. I had told them if they kept the same hours as I did, they might pick up some business from tourists looking for quick cash. I remembered wanting to buy a laptop from them before I went off to Europe. My uncle bought me a brand-new one and told me to never give them a dime. The bail bonds office was owned by a snowbird from Massachusetts who couldn't care less about anything but his skip tracers. I had thought about going into that line of work, but being a bouncer paid better.

"Fuck," I said, shaking my head. I really hoped the drug sales in my bar linked back to the Rivs. They might not have been the ones to burn down Uncle Johnny's, but they were getting more dangerous as they gained more power. Grier was probably asleep right now, otherwise I'd give him a call and see if we could speed things up and maybe meet tonight.

"It's the cost of doing business. And if Ginny was their mole inside the bar, or the other three missing idiots—four if you count your girlfriend's sister—"

"Are you really going there?" I tilted my head at him, but he ignored me.

"I'm just sayin' maybe the Rivs left you alone for two years because they had people inside making them money. And now those people are gone." Highway shrugged.

"It's a stretch. Dee left to become a hooker and Zeke followed her hoping to bring her home. But I'll ask her when I see her tomorrow." Since I had nothing better to do, I filled him in on what Jackie and I had found out. "If Paulie was the supplier, why did he leave? And leave the merchandise behind?" I shook my head. "None of this makes any fucking sense."

"Did you go to Paulie's place, since you seemed to be taking a tour of all your employees' digs? Am I next?" He put a hand over his chest. "I'll have to have the manservant polish the silverware."

I hadn't gone to Paulie's yet because I didn't want to spook him. I'd let Grier handle bringing him in for possession. I wanted to be out of it as much as possible.

"Just make sure you don't try and serve me some of that lemon shandy shit."

"I'm not a heathen," Highway said.

I gave him a noncommittal grunt and went back to glaring across the street. After another two hours, Highway and I headed back to the car where we took turns dozing and keeping an eye out for the inspector to call an all clear.

It was getting late and my mood wasn't improving. Even if there was even a miracle and this got sorted out, I'd be piss-poor company if I headed out to the Wynn tonight. I texted Jackie a few times to let her know that I wasn't going to make it. Either she was pissed off or asleep. With my luck it was probably the former. I'd deal with it tomorrow.

It took until dawn and I was too tired to give them the red ass that they deserved. I could open up as usual at noon for the lunch crowd. I left a message for Liu to bring in his cousins again and staggered up to my apartment to get a few hours of sleep.

CHAPTER THIRTEEN

Jackie Mitchell

I woke up this morning hugging a pasta bowl instead of a muscled bouncer with crazy hot tattoos. Fumbling for my phone, I saw it was past noon New York time, but still too early Las Vegas time to see Miles. I was ridiculously pleased to see he had texted last night and didn't blow me off. It was probably for the best that I had gotten a good night's sleep, even though my dreams left me feeling restless and needy. Maybe I could convince Miles to have another quickie in his office before we headed out to Pahrump.

Speaking of brothels, Chance didn't check in. I hoped that meant that they were having a good time. I also hoped that the bridegroom remained loyal to his bride. If I ever got engaged, there wouldn't be any chicken ranches in my husband-to-be's future. I might let him go to a strip club—if he let me dance in it.

Giggling to myself, I threw back the covers—mindful of the pasta bowls—and found that I was only slightly sore. Of course, the last thing my body wanted to do was dance. But I needed to get used to the idea of dancing every day, so I did some warmup exercises before doing my stripper routine that I had planned out. I never got to do my last two songs. Keeping with the Broadway theme, I had planned to do "You Can't Stop the Beat" from *Hairspray* and "One Night in Bangkok" from Chess. My costumes were so cute too. I wondered if Miles would change his mind about me dancing in the club and just let me just dance on stage and keep the tips, but not have to work the room.

Of course, that's what the other dancers had hated about Lisa. So maybe I should just stick to dancing in my hotel room for now. I flipped open my laptop to finish answering the pressing e-mails that I had blown off yesterday. Making myself a pot of coffee with the tiny machine in the room, I yawned.

My job was dull.

There. I admitted it. When I was in Manhattan, at least I could use the excuse that the city was exciting, and I was meeting and greeting directors and choreographers for new shows. It was fun to pitch my clients to them, even though I felt a twinge of jealousy when they got the contracts. The majority of my job, though, was reviewing contracts and researching opportunities for other people. I couldn't be too upset. I was making fifteen percent, but I'd rather be up on the stage.

For shits and giggles, I went online to the Las Vegas classifieds to see if there were any auditions this week. I didn't find any. I should have taken that as a sign, but instead I called my office back in New York. It didn't matter that it was a Saturday morning, the office never closed on the weekend.

"Zimmerman Agency," Mags, our receptionist said.

"Hi, Mags, it's me checking in from Sin City."

"We got two feet of snow dumped on us. Calling to rub it in?"

I hadn't been, but I pulled back the drape and gazed out into the sun and palm trees. I was glad I wasn't in New York. "Looks like it's going to hit ninety degrees today before noon."

"I'm hanging up now."

"Wait!" I leaned against the window, looking down at the Strip. It wasn't even noon yet, but there were still people out there hustling and working. It reminded me of New York. "I was wondering, do we have any connections out here? In the back of my mind I thought there was a production company that had been farming for showgirls a couple of years back. But I can't remember the name, otherwise I'd search it myself. Can you ask around and get back to me?"

"What's in it for me?" she teased.

"What do you want?" I said with a smile.

"I want you to put ten dollars on black twenty-two on the roulette table. If you win, we split it fifty-fifty."

"You're on."

"Give me fifteen minutes."

"Take all the time that you need." It was a silly idea anyway. Even if Mags found someone, I didn't have a client here. It was a long shot that Lisa would have tried to hook up with the same company. Of course, I wasn't asking on behalf of Lisa or my clients. I was thinking about what Miles had said and the remnants of my fantasy last night. Did I have what it took to ace an audition in a town where no one knew who I was?

Mags had hung up, but I still had the phone in my ear and was still looking out onto the busy street below. I could live here. It was warm and the city was exciting. I liked who I was in this place. And it was conveniently far away from my parents.

Feeling a little guilty about not calling him before now, I dialed my dad's number.

"Did you go broke?" was the first thing he said when he picked up.

"I haven't even stepped foot in a casino."

He made a disgusted sound. "You're wasting your life."

Unlike my mother, he was actually teasing me, and it made me smile. "Are you doing okay?"

"Your mother narced on me, didn't she? It was one beer."

"Just one?" I asked quietly.

"Cross my heart and hope to die."

I could picture him making the gesture.

"Why did you do it?" There wasn't any accusation in my voice. Just curiosity. He had hit rock bottom when I was in high school and spent the better part of a year in rehab. It had nearly torn our family apart. Lisa had taken Mom's side, while I was firmly convinced she had driven him to drink. I didn't want to think about that now. We had moved beyond it. Or at least I hoped we had.

He sighed. "I wanted to feel normal. I was playing cards with the guys and they were all drinking the first batch of winter ale. I just wanted a taste. I stopped at one bottle."

I was angrier with his friends than I was with him. They'd been playing cards every Friday all my life. They knew the history.

"I'm proud of you. It must not have been easy to stop at one."

"Well, that was all they had," he admitted. "Your mother caught me because I bought a six-pack coming home and tried to sneak it in."

I winced. "Well, I hope you learned your lesson."

"Yeah," he said. "Leave it in the car until she falls asleep."

"Da-ad," I groaned, but I knew he was just joking. I heard my mother in the background.

"Is that Lisa?"

"Tell her yes and that she's doing fine."

"Is that the truth?"

I hesitated too long in my answer and my mother came on the line. "Lisa, honey. I've been worried sick."

"It's me," I said, resting my forehead against the window. I should be given brownie points for not banging my head against it.

"Well, where is she?"

"She's left Las Vegas."

"Good. There's too much temptation in that town."

She wasn't wrong. My mind wandered over to Miles. I wanted to spend a lot more time with him, but I was on vacation this week and he wasn't. I needed to understand that. It's just that he made me feel like I was important to him, a priority in his life. That was more seductive to me than his talented tongue. Well, maybe not. I had to have a little more of that to make sure.

"Where is she?" my mother repeated.

Good question. "I've tracked her down to a . . . um . . . bar in Pahrump, Nevada." Here's hoping she didn't Google it. "I'm going out there today."

"Pahrump? I've never heard of it. I wonder if it's the new indie dance scene."

"Maybe," I drawled out.

"So you're going to see her today."

I doubted it. "Hopefully, but she's not making this easy. She knows I'm here. She could pick up the phone and have a five-minute phone conversation with me."

"If she's getting your messages," my mother said ominously. "Maybe she lost her phone." That seemed to brighten her day. And since it was better than telling her that Lisa had gone from a bartender to an exotic dancer, and that my current theory was she was now a legal prostitute, I let her believe that.

"I'll call you when I find her," I said.

I took a quick shower and got dressed. Mags called back while I was eating breakfast in the buffet in the casino after losing ten bucks on black twenty-two. It had come up red twelve. So close and yet so far.

"Sorry it took so long," Mags said.

"Bad news. We lost."

"Easy come, easy go." I could picture her shrugging. "Anyway, I've got good news and bad news."

"Hit me."

"See, you're getting into the casino frame of mind. The bad news is I couldn't find the company you were thinking of."

"Yeah, me neither."

"But there is a company that works with the Zimmerman office in LA. They're looking for showgirls for a new show based on *Travesty*."

"*Travesty*?"

"It's the new video game that all the kids are playing. It's a cross between Clue, Fortnite, and Dance Revolution."

"Okay," I said, trying to picture that in my head and failing.

"They're auditioning all week at the new hotel casino on the Strip, the Odyssey. It's a video game-themed casino."

"Really?" I chewed on my bacon. "Can you get me in?"

"For who? Lisa?"

I froze. I couldn't very well say that it was for me. "Yeah, Lisa."

"You found her? How is she? How's her knee?"

I didn't like to lie, but I was having a hard time digging myself out of this one. "Yup, she's been bartending and trying to find herself out here. She was stripping at one of the local clubs."

"Get the fuck out!" Mags screamed.

That was going to get all over the office. It was cheap, but it was going to keep the interest off of me.

"Yeah, so her knee is doing well. I think she's out here for the time being so I figured why not see if I could get her a job." I hated lying to Mags, but it was harmless. No one would have to know I went on the audition myself.

"You're always working," Mags said. "All right, let me see if they can fit Lisa in. I'll call you back."

I was surprised that my hand was shaking when I drained my coffee in one long sip. This was ridiculous. I wasn't really going to masquerade as my sister at a dance audition. They would know the minute I walked in that I wasn't her based on the headshots and résumé Zimmerman would fax over. This was just Las Vegas Jackie poking fun at New York Jackie.

Mags called back immediately. "Can you get Lisa there in the next hour?"

I gulped. "Sh-shit. I mean sure."

"Good. They'll be going over the combinations to all the dancers then. It'll take about an hour. Then they'll give them a half hour to practice and then they'll start calling the dancers on stage to audition."

Oh God.

"What kind of dancing are they looking for?" I was shell-shocked, but my mouth went on autopilot, asking the questions I normally would if I was actually sending Lisa.

"Hip-hop, modern, but don't be surprised if they ask to see a kick line. It is Vegas after all."

"What can you tell me about the decision-makers?" I murmured, my mind going a million directions at once.

"The casting director is Simi Pierce. Tell Lisa to wear

something formfitting. They're going to want to see her body. And have her wear shorts. They want to see her legs."

"How do I get to the audition?" I cleared my throat. I had to get my head on straight.

"Pull around the back of the Odyssey casino into the employees' lot, and tell the guard you're there to audition for *Travesty*. Go into stage door C and tell them you're with the Zimmerman Agency."

"Got it," I whispered.

"Break a leg," Mags said.

I was going to throw up. No. I was just not going to the audition. I wasted five valuable minutes arguing with myself. Then I ran up to my room to get changed into a tight T-shirt and my stripper shorts. I was not wearing the butt floss. No way. No how.

Miles texted when I was in the car. My phone read the text to me over the rental car's speakers.

Good Morning, beautiful. Can you get here around three and we can drive up to Pahrump?

It was ten a.m. now.

Instead of texting him back, I called. I needed to hear his voice. He was the only one I could tell this to without dealing with backlash and baggage. The hands-free dialed out for me.

"Hi," I said when he picked up. "Do you have a minute?"

"Is everything all right?"

"I'm not sure."

"Do you need me to come over?"

I smiled. "I needed you last night."

"I'm sorry. The jerks at the gas company took their sweet-ass time. It was after dawn by the time they cleared the place."

"I wouldn't have minded being woken up by you." At a stoplight, I stared at my nails critically. I should have gotten a mani-pedi the moment I arrived. Hopefully, no one would notice.

"I wouldn't have been at my best."

I shivered at the rough tone of his voice.

"You could come over now," he said. "I'll make you some breakfast."

"I've already eaten."

"Perfect. Then I'll have you for breakfast."

Swallowing hard, I shifted in the driver's seat. "Sounds great, but I'm going to have to take a rain check."

"You better not be in Pahrump already," he growled.

"I'm not. I'm actually going to the Odyssey casino right now."

"I didn't think they were open."

"They're not, but they're auditioning for their new show *Travesty* and . . . I'm going to give it a shot." I had to lower the volume at his whoop of encouragement.

"You're going to blow them all away," he said.

"That's the plan. If I can stop shaking."

"I wish I could be there to cheer you on."

Damn, had anyone ever said that to me? "I'm scared."

"You've got nothing to worry about. You know how these things go. You've done auditions before. Just go out there and show them that star quality that you showed us last night. Only keep your clothes on."

I had to laugh. "They wouldn't blink an eye if I went out there naked."

"I doubt that. You're going to slay them, sweetheart. What are you going to do if you get the part?"

"I won't. They'll do a callback." At least, I thought they would. "Anyway, I can't think about that right now. I just have to get through the audition first."

"I'll be here waiting for you. You can do this, Jackie. You're an amazing dancer."

If I didn't throw up or trip or break an ankle learning the combination.

"Say something, gorgeous, so I know you're still breathing."

"I'm here."

"You've got this. Put Lisa and all the other bullshit out of your mind and take the stage like you did yesterday."

"I've got to be Las Vegas Jackie, not New York Jackie," I muttered.

"Right. Whatever that means."

"Okay, thanks Miles." I took a deep breath and straightened my shoulders.

"Thanks for what?"

"For talking me off the ledge. I needed that."

"Always."

Always. I'd known him less than a week and he'd supported me more than my family had my entire life. If I wasn't careful, I was going to fall for him hard. Who was I kidding? If bouncers had wall calendars like Australian soccer players, Miles would be my Mr. February.

"I can't wait to see you today," I said.

"Come as soon as you're free."

"I hope to," I said as flirtatiously as I could.

"Mmm, you will," he promised and then hung up.

Great, now I was all hot and bothered. Following Mags's instructions, I parked in the Odyssey's employee parking lot. I checked my makeup. I was wearing dark lipstick and went light on everything else. I didn't want to risk looking like a raccoon or sweating my foundation all over my white T-shirt.

"Just another audition," I told myself in the rearview mirror. "It means nothing. It's not like you're going to take the job. You're here to cross something off your bucket list." I looked up at the casino. "Even if they don't call me back, I can still say I danced on stage in Vegas." Of course, I'd done that last night. But this was a little more official. I wouldn't have to take my clothes off.

Getting out of the car, I made my way to stage door C and met up with a bored-looking man wearing a headset and carrying a clipboard.

"Name," he droned.

"Jackie Mitchell from the Zimmerman Agency." I held my breath as he frowned at his list.

"Got a Lisa Mitchell."

"Lisa?" I deliberately raised my voice. "Oh no. That's my sister. They sent the wrong file." I put an edge of hysteria in my voice.

He held up a hand and winced. "You have your portfolio?"

"I can e-mail it." I showed him my phone.

"Fine," he droned again. He crossed off Lisa and put Jackie on his list. "Send it here." He pointed to the address at the top of the clipboard.

"Sent," I said breathlessly. I hoped this was going to work.

He opened up his own phone and after a moment nodded. "Down the hall. Third room on the left. Stash your bag and phone in the locker and then head out to the stage. Take a right out of the dressing room and keep going. You'll find it."

I was in. My knees wobbled as I went to the locker room. Time for Las Vegas Jackie to shine—or fail.

CHAPTER FOURTEEN

Miles Carvello

I was happy for Jackie. It was pure selfishness that I hoped she got the job and stayed awhile in Vegas. The past week had been the best I'd had in a long time. She made things seem fresh and fun again. She reminded me that there was a world outside of Dalton's. I was looking forward to seeing her reaction to the Moondust Cherry Ranch, but brothels weren't really my thing. While I could see the appeal of the lack of strings attached when quick sex was a transaction, I imagined it got old really fast. I could save myself a grand by jacking off to online porn and get the same satisfaction.

In my experience with cathouses and the women who worked them, there were three types of hookers. The ones there to make as much money as possible in a short period of time gave good customer service, but nickel-and-dimed everything. The damaged ones looked for love and acceptance and got what they could from pleasing the customer.

They did whatever it took to give the client a good time and keep them spending money because it made the house happy and it made her feel valued. And then there were the ones that liked sex and getting paid for it. They got paid for having fun. The last type were few and far between, no matter what hype the madam and her girls told you. And after listening to their mothers, I'd put Dee as a number one and Jackie's sister as a number two—if she had made the jump to prostitute.

Grier was late and, while I appreciated that his undercover status made his schedule flexible, I wanted our business over and done with by the time Jackie came back from her audition. I knew she would be eager to get on the road to find out about her sister, but I was eager to spend some time making love to her first. And it seemed like she felt the same.

Liu and his cousins were in the kitchen making something delicious and I hoped Jackie wouldn't think I was a cheapskate if I recommended we eat here before heading out. I wanted more intimate moments with her, like being in my apartment alone instead of surrounded by a hundred other people in a restaurant.

Miranda was lazily swaying around the pole when I went out to check on things. Grier was there at the front table, nursing a beer and a plate of nachos.

"You could have texted me that you were here."

"I wanted to enjoy the show," he said, not taking his eyes off Miranda.

Miranda couldn't dance worth a squat, but her body was banging. The music was low, and the lights were high because it was early in the day.

"You might want to have a talk with her, though. She's flashed me the goods a few times."

I glared up at Miranda. She was looking at a two-thousand-dollar fine if she didn't keep her bits covered. "Dip you tip her?"

"A twenty both times." He grinned at me. "So you know I won't bust her because that could be entrapment."

"Stop leading my dancers into temptation."

"I think I'm in love. Lighten up."

"I can't. Did you hear what happened last night?" I thanked Jilly, his waitress, when she came over with my usual club soda and lime.

"Yeah, from what I gathered some asshole sprayed something that smelled like gas and people panicked and you got shut down." Grier couldn't take his eyes off Miranda. I was pretty sure she wasn't going to flash him again while I was sitting there.

"Let's go back into my office and I'll tell you why I think that might be related to a few findings I've had this week."

Grier held up another twenty and Miranda hopped down from the stage. It never failed to amaze me that she did that in five-inch heels.

"Do you want a lap dance?" she purred.

"Later." He tucked the bill into her G-string and if his fingers lingered a bit, neither one of them minded.

I headed over to my office. Grier knew the way. I had a moment to wish Jackie were here as I sat behind my desk. Grier walked in a few minutes later and closed the door behind him.

"Why am I here?" he asked, sitting in the armchair across from me. He still had half a beer, so I tossed him a coaster while I told him about Ginny selling drugs to frat boys in the dressing room and finding the stash in Paulie's locker.

"Let me see the haul."

I opened the safe and handed over the pistol and the drugs. "This was what I found in the locker." Grier frowned and turned the bags over and over while he looked at them. He opened the one with the pills and squinted at the capsule.

Then he took the powder and tentatively sniffed. Turning away, he sneezed into his shoulder.

"You made me come out here special for this shit? At least Miranda made it worth the trip," he said.

"What are you talking about?"

"There's not enough weed here to make a profit. The powder could have traces of coke in it, but it's mostly talc and I'm pretty sure these are over-the-counter allergy meds." He waved the bag of pills.

"What the crap?"

"I'll run a trace on the pistol, but I don't think it will give us anything. Someone was either setting Paulie up or is fucking with you. Let me see Ginny's stash."

Getting the smaller baggies out of the safe, I looked them over and then tossed them to him. It seemed like the same shit to me. "Why would they be setting Paulie up?"

"To get heat taken off of them. Because Paulie pissed them off. There's a whole host of reasons." He pocketed the pistol.

I watched as Grier compared the two sets of drugs.

"This shit is real. I'll see if I can trace them back to a known batch." Leaning back in his chair. "You shouldn't have fired Ginny."

"I wasn't thinking. I was pissed."

"Is there any way she'd come back?"

I made a face. "Maybe if I kissed her ass and begged."

"Do it."

"Why?"

"Because she'll behave for a few weeks and then get right back into it. And then I'll send a frat boy of my own choosing to buy from her and we'll see if she'll make a deal."

"You can pick her up right now based on this stuff, right? I caught her in the act. That's possession and intent to sell right there."

Grier held up a hand. "Settle down, Columbo. It's not that easy. It would be your word against hers. You didn't actually see money exchange hands, did you?"

"No," I admitted.

"Did you get the little frat asshole's name and number?"

"No."

"Then a competent lawyer would argue that the drugs were his and she'd walk."

"Fuck." I rubbed my hand over my face.

"Get Ginny back here and we can try again." Grier got up to leave. I walked him to the door. Scrolling through my phone, I hoped I had deleted Ginny's number so I wouldn't have to call her. Unfortunately, I wasn't that organized.

Opening the door for him, I said, "I'll give her a call and grovel."

"Do that. And if you get any more like this," he shook the baggies, "give me a call. Oh, excuse me, Miss."

I looked up from dialing Ginny and saw Jackie standing there, stunned as Grier moved around her and went back into club.

"How did it go?" I asked.

She turned on her heel and stormed away.

"Jackie, wait!"

Ginny took that moment to answer the phone. "I knew you'd call."

Fuck. I wanted to go after Jackie, but I needed to get on Ginny's good side first. "Yeah, look. I'm sorry. I was a dick that night. If you still want a job, you got it." *That ought to be enough, right?*

"Just like that?"

"Don't break my balls." I watched as Jackie stormed past Grier and out of the club. Fuck.

"I don't want to work Sundays. I want prime time Friday and Saturday."

"Fine," I bit out, telling myself I was doing this so Grier would share information with me.

"And I want to negotiate your percentage," she said.

"My percentage is fair," I said. If word got out that I was willing to drop my cut, I'd be in a load of trouble. "I don't charge a house fee or make you tip out."

Although most of the dancers did tip the bus staff, DJs, and bouncers at the end of the night.

"You owe me for being mean to me," she wheedled.

I had to get this bitch off the phone and go after Jackie. "If you want the job be here Friday night. If not, don't. You're getting the same fifty-fifty split as all the other girls, though."

"I'll think about it." She hung up on me.

I rushed through the bar after Jackie.

————

Jackie Mitchell

Oh my God. Miles was a drug dealer. I barely made it to my car before I started to cry. How could I have been so stupid? I pulled out into traffic and headed back to the Strip. I'd go to Pahrump on my own. I should have known better than to get so involved before I knew a thing about Miles aside from the fact he fucked like a Greek god. I didn't even get a chance to tell him about the audition. I realized I was too upset to drive, so I pulled into a parking garage until I got under control.

Did Lisa leave Dalton's because she didn't want to be involved with the drug scene?

Miles was blowing up my phone, but I didn't want to deal with him right now. Damn it. All I wanted was to ride the buzz of my audition for a little while and have some hot sex with a man I really liked before I had to drive two hours to track down Lisa. I didn't even know him. And I had no one to blame, but Las Vegas Jackie.

My stomach growled loudly, reminding me I hadn't eaten since breakfast. I'd danced my ass off at the audition, so those calories were long gone. Getting out of the car, I decided to grab a late lunch and a few cups of coffee before heading out. Walking down the Strip, I barely registered the sights, but when a convertible started beeping the horn at me it jolted me out of my thoughts. At first glance it was filled with obnoxious, but gorgeous men. I did a double take until I recognized Chance at the wheel. He pulled to the curb, pissing off everyone on the road, but he didn't care.

"Want a ride, luv?" he asked, grinning at me.

"Are all Australian men hot? Is it like a requirement for living in the country?"

"Yes." He nodded. "Get in."

"I don't think there's room for me."

"I'll make one of these wankers walk." Then he looked at me closer. "Have you been crying?"

"No," I said.

Chance put the car in park and hopped out.

"You can't park there," I said.

The guys in the car did vehicular musical chairs and the new driver took off while the others gave Chance obscene gestures and called him vulgar names. He flipped them off as they sped away.

"They just stranded you," I said.

"I'll catch up." He took hold of my elbow. "Now tell me who made you cry so I can kick his arse."

"Miles," I said.

"He's a tough bloke," Chance said. "And he hits like a

fucking sledgehammer. Before I go toe-to-toe with him, do you mind telling me what he did?"

"I don't know where to start," I said helplessly.

"Where are you heading?"

"I was going to get something to eat."

"Bonzer. I know the perfect place. Do you like drag queens?"

"Who doesn't?"

A few minutes later, we were being serenaded by dual Chers singing Abba. I had an enormous iced coffee in front of me with shaved chocolate chips and real whipped cream. Our burgers and fries were on the way.

"Did you find Lisa?" I asked, wishing there were a way I could inject the caffeine directly into my veins. But that made me think of Miles and that horrid scene at Dalton's.

"Not a trace, but I think that might be a good thing."

"I'm heading up there today to see if I can get a lead on where she went. Miles was going to come with me for moral support." I looked up at Chance hopefully. "I don't suppose you want to tag along."

He shook his head. "I can't. We're going to throw axes and joust."

"Sounds like a great time."

"I'm in it for the turkey legs the size of dinner platters."

The food came quickly, and I was dunking a thick steak fry into a puddle of ketchup when Chance said, "So tell me about Miles."

I quickly stuffed the fry in my mouth to give me time to compose myself while I chewed. "I went to Dalton's and caught him making a drug deal."

"That doesn't sound like Miles," Chance said. "He's clean and hates the stuff. At least he did in 'Straya."

"People change," I said, drowning my sorrows in the iced coffee,

"Tell me exactly what you saw." Chance attacked his burger like he hadn't eaten in weeks.

"Miles and some other guy were leaving his office. The other guy was carrying some baggies. I saw pills and weed. He told Miles to call him if he got more of the good stuff."

"What was Miles doing?"

"He was on the phone. I heard him say something along the lines that he had to grovel to someone."

"I can see why you thought a drug deal was going down, but there could be another explanation," Chance said. "What did he say happened?"

"I don't know. I ran out of there."

"Has he called?"

"Yeah." I looked into my purse.

"You owe it to him to hear him out."

"Why?" I said. I didn't want him to lie, and worse I didn't want to believe some half-ass story because I still wanted the bastard.

"In all of the time I've known Miles, he's never dated an exotic dancer. And I've seen them throw themselves at him."

That didn't surprise me.

"I've also never seen him come to personally escort a dancer who wasn't in trouble out of a VIP room, so I'm going to go out on a limb and say I think you've gotten under his skin in a good way. And the way you're feeling makes me think you're in the same boat."

I nodded, not trusting myself to speak.

"He's a good bloke. Give him a chance to explain what you saw. If you still want me to knock him around after, I'll give it a go."

"That won't be necessary." I pulled out my phone. Three missed calls and two texts.

Where are you? Why did you leave? and *Call me.*

I showed them to Chance.

"He's a man of few words. Put the poor bastard out of his misery. Tell him you'll be over after we've finished lunch." He checked his phone. "Can you drop me off at the Rio first though? The boys are hitting the tables and I'm feeling lucky."

CHAPTER FIFTEEN

Miles Carvello

Jackie's text said she'd pick me up in front of Dalton's in a half hour and then she didn't pick up the phone or respond to any of my texts. I was trying not to be pissed, but it wasn't working. Thirty minutes later on the dot, she pulled up in her rental car.

"We're taking my car," I told her.

She opened her mouth to argue with me, but must have seen the look on my face. "Fine."

Backing out of my parking spot, I gave her enough room to pull in and then waited for her to get in the car before ripping into her.

"What the fuck was that all about?" I had preset the Moondust Cherry Ranch into the GPS, so I didn't need to think about directions. I pulled into traffic and glared at her out of the corner of my eye.

"Miles, are you selling drugs?"

"The fuck?" I whipped a glance at her. "Is that what you

think you saw?"

"What *did* I see?"

I shook my head and tried to put a simmer on my temper. Normally I wouldn't tell anyone about Grier, but Jackie was leaving in less than two weeks. "That was an undercover cop trying to get a hold on the drug trade this side of the Strip. I'd appreciate it if you don't mention that bit of information to anyone. It could literally cost him his life."

"That's a convenient story," she said.

I shook my head. "You can believe me or not. I don't give a fuck."

"I want to believe you," Jackie said. She placed her hand on my arm. I shook her off, still too pissed at her to want her touch. I knew this was a bad idea. I should have gently tossed her fine ass out of my club instead of letting her shake it on stage and I definitely shouldn't have fucked her over a desk. I should have taken my time with her in bed. Because that was all I could think about now. How it was all fucked up and it would have been so damn good.

"You don't have to take me to Pahrump," she said quietly.

I pulled over to the side of the road, amidst the blaring of horns. "Do you want me to go with you or not?"

"Yes. Yes, I want you to come with me to Pahrump. Yes, I want to believe you're not a drug dealer. And yes, I still want to fuck your brains out."

My lips twitched. "You couldn't have led off with that last one?" And just like that the anger simmered down to a mild irritation. I got back on the road.

"Here's the thing," Jackie said, and I couldn't wait for what was going to come next. "We missed a few steps in our courtship. I'm not complaining, because I liked what happened. But I know nothing about you that hasn't come from the Internet. How would I know you weren't a drug dealer?"

"Fair enough." I shrugged. "The Internet has most of it. What holes do you want me to fill in?"

"Are we still talking about sex? Because all of them."

"All?" I drawled. The day was looking up. Another notch of tension eased in my back. Maybe this situation wasn't completely fucked up.

"Why did you come back to Las Vegas? You looked like you were living the dream in Ibiza, London, and Mykonos." Jackie kicked off her shoes and put her feet on my dashboard. "I bet you saw a lot of exotic dancers."

I swatted her feet down, avoiding the question. "That's dangerous. If we get into an accident, your dance career is over."

"Danger is my middle name," she said.

"Is it?"

"No it's Aida. My mom gave us Broadway middle names. Lisa's middle name is Pippin."

"You got lucky."

"One of the few perks of being born first." Jackie eased the seat back. "Have you got a middle name?"

"No. My parents weren't too concerned with me. My uncle Johnny raised me for the most part. You would have liked him. He had a weird sense of humor and he loved blondes."

She was quiet for a moment. "When did he pass away?"

"About two years ago. He died in a fire when some assholes burned down his club."

"That's awful." Jackie gasped and touched my arm again. This time I let her keep it there.

"I rebuilt over the spot. Dalton was his last name. His place was called Uncle Johnny's Gentlemen's Club. Full nude. He didn't serve alcohol. I worked there as a kid."

"Your parents didn't mind?"

"If it didn't involve cards or dice, my parents didn't care

about much. I don't even know if they're still alive. I doubt it. They didn't come to Uncle Johnny's funeral."

"Have you ever tried to find them?"

"I haven't seen them in twenty years. I don't even remember what they look like."

"I'm sorry."

"I couldn't care less about them. It's my uncle I want justice for. They never caught the people who set the fire. The cops didn't even know where to start looking. The first thing I did when I got here was research the local gangs. That's how I met Grier."

"Let me guess. You saved him from a beat down too."

I gave her a strange look.

"Chance said you took a bottle in the arm for him."

"That was a long time ago." I shrugged it off. "Anyway, the gangs were in a turf war. The cops figured Uncle Johnny's was just collateral damage."

"What do you think?"

"I think the bail bondsman and the pawnshop across the street weren't touched because they paid protection. Uncle Johnny didn't. I think the other places on the street laundered money or let the gang sell out of their stores. Uncle Johnny didn't allow any shit in his bar. People were banned for life if they brought in drugs, prostitution or if someone started a fight. He had enemies. It could have been one of them."

"Do you have any trouble like that?"

"Not so much. The local gang calls themselves the Rivs after the Riviera Casino that was torn down in 2015. Their leader, Leonidas, and I bumped heads a few years ago but I don't think he was responsible for burning down my uncle's bar."

"Why?"

"At the time, he didn't have the clout to pull it off. Nowadays, it's not his style. He's more a bullets and shanking type of guy."

"Do you think it was the mob?" Jackie asked.

"Possibly, but not likely. Uncle Johnny's had a small local following and he liked it that way. He wouldn't have attracted the attention of the bigger families."

"It must be frustrating for you."

"I thought I'd have an answer by now, yeah. But I like my club. It's nice to have a home of my own. Don't get me wrong, traveling all over the world for ten years was great. But when I lost Uncle Johnny, all I could think of was that I should have been here. Maybe, if I had been, he wouldn't have died."

"You don't know that. You might have died with him." Jackie's voice caught.

I gave her a reassuring smile. "I'm a lot tougher than I look. Anyway, I help Grier in his job, and he keeps an ear out. The trail grows colder each day, but I know one day I'll get Uncle Johnny justice."

"I believe you," she said, and leaned her head on my shoulder.

"How did the audition go?" I asked.

She sat up straight again. "It was awesome. I think I did okay. At least I didn't embarrass myself. The combo was giving me a hard time, but I think I nailed it when I was up there by myself. Anyway, they'll call if they're interested— which means I'll never hear from them again."

"Think positive."

"I'm positive I won't get a callback. But it doesn't matter. I did it and I'm glad I went." She leaned over and kissed my cheek.

"What's that for?"

"For putting up with my shit." She gave me another. "That one's for giving a shit about the audition."

"Like I told you, anytime." I waited for a stop light, turned her face to mine, and kissed her lips.

The honking told me the light had changed and I reluctantly pulled back. She seemed as breathless as me. Jackie chattered on about the dance routine and the choreography. It went over my head, but it made the drive go by easier. She helped me stop thinking of how I fucked up by letting my temper get to me when I fired Ginny, instead of playing smart and letting Grier handle it. Being with Jackie reminded me of the good times I had in Ibiza, when the worst problem I had was whether to wear my Bulgari watch or my Rolex. I had hocked both of them to pay rent on Dalton's a year ago. I didn't miss them, but I did miss cruising with a beautiful woman at my side.

"Are you sure this is it?" Jackie asked as we pulled into the Moondust Cherry Ranch parking lot. It didn't look like much from the outside, basically several double wide trailers linked together into a ring.

"What were you expecting?"

"Something a little fancier."

"They don't need to be fancy on the outside."

I got out of the car and opened the door for her. I figured taking her to a chicken ranch lost me gentleman points, so I wanted to make up for it.

"Have you . . . have you ever been here before?" she asked, looking up at me with her big green eyes.

"No, but what you're really asking me is if I've ever been to a brothel before, right?"

"More like do you have a frequent fucker card."

She surprised a laugh out of me. "No. The last time I frequented a house of ill repute I was eighteen. I had just graduated from high school and that was my Uncle Johnny's present to me."

"How . . . sweet?" Jackie said tentatively as we walked up

to the front door. Sounds of loud bass lines and laughter drifted out through the door.

I snorted. "I would have rather he'd given me the thousand bucks."

"A thousand?" She gaped at me. "What the hell did you get for that?"

I had to think about it. "I got a hand job. A blow job. Body touching privileges and a quick lay."

"Did you order that off the menu?"

"Yes," I said seriously. "That's how it goes. It took about an hour."

"A thousand bucks an hour sure beats two fifty." Jackie inhaled a shaky breath.

"I'm not sure how much the house cut is, but they also pay out to the taxi and limo drivers. I have no idea what the takeaway is. If Broadway didn't like grinding in the VIP room, your sister would never do what these girls do all day."

"I hope you're right." Jackie wiped her hands on her skirt. "Dee said just to come in and ask for her."

"Don't be nervous." I gave her a quick hug. "I'm here. Whatever we find out, we'll handle it together."

She buried her face in my chest and gripped me tightly. "I've never had someone say that to me. I've always had to handle Lisa's bullshit on my own. I can't tell you what it means that you're here with me."

Leaning in to whisper in her ear, I gave her earlobe a quick nibble. "Besides, you might enjoy yourself."

"I'm not expensing a grand in a whorehouse. I'm pushing the limit to what my mother is going to reimburse me for, as it is." With a deep breath, she pushed away. "Okay, let's find out what fuckery my sister has got herself into now."

"That's the spirit."

I rang the doorbell and slung my arm around her. "Don't leave my side."

"You can bet your sweet ass I won't."

The madam opened the door. She had platinum blond hair that was pulled back into a severe bun. She was dressed in a conservative suit and her welcoming smile faded when she saw Jackie. "Couples night out?" she asked.

"Dee told us to come by," Jackie said, holding on to me for dear life.

The madam's face brightened a bit and she stepped away from the door. "Come in then. I'll check her availability."

I think Jackie would have rather waited on the doorstep, but I ushered her inside. In the parlor area women in various state of undress draped themselves over men or burgundy red velvet couches. Jackie was the only nonworking girl there.

A woman dressed up like an angel came up to us and smiled. "Are you looking for a party?"

"We're here for Dee," I said when Jackie just gawked.

"I'm Angelique." She trailed a finger down my shirt. "If you change your mind, I'll be in the bar." She gestured behind her. In the bar was a wide-screen television playing a porno. There were men with women on their laps. Others were playing pool, and some were drinking and staring at the movie intently.

"This is super awkward," Jackie said.

The bell rang again, and I pulled Jackie away from the door. "Let's sit down." I picked one of the couches that faced away from the bar and hauled her on my lap. She settled in with a dazed expression on her face. Leaning in, she whispered in my ear, "Do they think we're going to have a threesome with Dee?"

"Yes. And I'm pretty sure we're going to have to pay for Dee's time."

"That bitch," Jackie gasped. "I figured we'd talk to her between shifts."

"It doesn't look that way. Let me negotiate."

"Don't let her screw us." Jackie snorted when she realized what she'd said.

The madam had let in a group of men in cowboy hats and boots, wearing rodeo shirts. She pressed a buzzer and the unattached women lined up. More girls came from the back rooms. They were dressed in everything from lingerie to black latex to fetish costumes. The cowboys each picked a girl and went off with them down various hallways. The other ones worked the room.

Angelique circled back around to us, her wings dragging on the floor and dropping white feathers.

"I think she's molting," Jackie muttered in my ear.

"Dee's going to be about another fifteen minutes. I could warm you up if you want. We could have a lot of fun."

"Can we talk?" Jackie said.

"Oh honey, I'm a great listener. Why don't we go to my room and see if we can come to an arrangement?"

Jackie looked at me and I shrugged. "It's your money."

"I like an independent woman." Angelique smiled and led us out of the parlor.

"Do you know what you're doing?" I muttered to her.

"It's just like the VIP room. We're going to get hustled for drinks and I'm going to get some information."

"Okay." I was either the luckiest guy in the world or the biggest idiot for letting her do this.

Angelique didn't bring us into her bedroom, like I'd thought she would. It was more of a waiting room with couches and a thick shag rug. There was a coffee table with various plastic wrapped sex toys. Jackie sat next to me on the couch while Angelique sank to the floor at our feet. She handed Jackie a laminated menu and I glanced over. I hid a grin when I saw that it was a list of services and prices. Jackie gently set it on the table and said, "How much to just ask some questions?"

"A hundred dollars for fifteen minutes. Just talk. No touching."

"Deal," Jackie said and went to shake her hand. "Oh right, no touching." Pulling her arm back, she dug into her purse and handed Angelique a hundred-dollar bill.

"Thank you. I'll be right back. Can I get you something to drink?"

"A Diet Coke?" Jackie asked.

"Nothing for me." I needed to keep my wits about me.

"Where's she going?" Jackie asked.

"To log in the money."

Jackie nodded and within five minutes Angelique was back with a Diet Coke. Jackie gulped about half of it down. "Thanks," she said. "Do you know Lisa Mitchell? She might be going by the name Broadway. She was bartending here a few weeks ago." Out came Lisa's headshot.

"Oh yeah, I remember her. She got pissed off that she wasn't making what she thought she should in tips. Cheri tossed her out on her ass after a week."

"Who's Cheri?"

"She's the madam and no she won't talk with you. She's too busy."

"Do you know where Lisa went?"

Angelique shook her head. "I couldn't tell you."

I wondered if that was couldn't or wouldn't. I kept my mouth shut for now. Angelique didn't ask why we were so interested in Lisa. Either she didn't care, or she knew Dee was going to spill the beans anyway so the information was not a secret.

"Did she have a boyfriend?" I asked. "Or a guy who would visit her regularly?"

"Parker," Angelique said. "He dropped her off and picked her up. We tried to get him to stay awhile, but he wasn't interested. Kind of like you." She pouted at me.

"Sorry," I said.

"Your loss."

"I'm sure it is." I tried to be polite, but I got jabbed in the ribs again. I narrowed my eyes at Jackie. There was definitely going to be some payback.

"Anyway," Jackie said, clearing her throat. "Did you catch Parker's last name?"

"No." Angelique flicked her eyes to the clock.

"What did he look like?" Jackie spoke faster.

"He was tall, handsome in a silver fox way. He dressed nice. You could tell he had money."

"Did she seem afraid of him?"

"No, she was more afraid of losing him."

Cocking her head, Jackie said, "What do you mean?"

"She was super possessive and jealous. On her breaks she would call to check up on him."

"How did he treat her?"

"Protective, maybe even overprotective."

"How?" Jackie leaned forward.

"He was careful around her, like she was made of glass. He'd put his arm around her when she left with him after her shift and he made it a point to walk her to the door at the start of the shift."

"Did she ever talk about him?"

"Yeah, just that he was going to make her a star. As soon as he got his show going."

Jackie zeroed in on that like a target. "What kind of show?"

"Some dance review. Between you and me, I think he was stringing her along. You know the type. 'Stick with me kid, and I'll take you away from all this.'" Her lips twisted in a sneer and she rolled her eyes. "I bet she was financing that show and that's why she got her panties in a bunch about the tips. You've got time for one more question."

"Did Lisa ever . . . Did she . . ." Jackie couldn't say it.

"Did she join you guys in the lineup and hustle for blow jobs and quick fucks?" I filled in.

Angelique burst out laughing and wouldn't stop. Two girls poked their heads into the waiting room to see what was going on. She waved them off.

"I think that's a no," I said. Jackie sagged against me in relief.

"Thanks for that," Angelique wiped her eyes with the back of her hand. "Damn it. I'm going to have to redo my eyeliner. No. Lisa slung drinks. She was stone-faced and never smiled. She was so unfriendly that if she hadn't been fired over the bullshit about her tips, Cheri was going to put her in the back doing laundry and working in the kitchen where she didn't scare the clients." Angelique got up. "Dee should be wrapping it up by now. I'll send her in to get you. Don't do anything I wouldn't do." She blew us a kiss.

"Thank you. You've been really helpful," Jackie said.

"I aim to please." Angelique sashayed out.

"That should put your mind at ease," I said when we were alone.

Jackie pressed her palms to her flushed face. "It all seems so stupid now that I thought Lisa would become a prostitute. I don't know what I was thinking."

"You were trying to follow her thought patterns and since she's still ditching your calls, you had to take some wild guesses."

"She's had us all worried. I hope this Parker guy isn't stringing her along. But I guess she's living with him. Maybe Dee will have more information."

"Come here," I said and hauled her back onto my lap. "We're getting close to finding your sister."

Jackie wrapped her arms around my neck. "I can't wait for this to be over so I can spend some more time with you."

I grinned. "I was hoping you felt the same way I did." I actually wanted her longer than this vacation would last. "And who knows, if you get the showgirl job . . ."

"Shh," she said, pressing her fingers to my mouth. "You'll jinx it."

I kissed her fingers. "So what do you think of your first brothel?"

Glancing around the room, she shrugged. "It's not very sexy or romantic."

"To be fair, you're not their demographic."

She was quiet for a full minute, so I knew something was up. "What's going on in that head of yours?" I asked.

"Was the woman your uncle rented for you pretty?"

We were heading into the danger zone, I could sense it. "I honestly don't remember, but I'm sure she was."

"Why didn't you ever come back?"

"I like things to go more natural. And I love kissing. Most working girls don't like that."

"I get it," Jackie said snuggling into me. "Kissing is intimate. By holding back, they can separate work from fun." She turned my head and kissed me openmouthed, slow and sweet. I rubbed my hand over her back. She tasted like mint and our tongues slid along each other. It was easy to get lost in her mouth on mine.

"You guys are going to have to pay for it if you keep it up."

I bit back a groan. "Hi, Dee," I said.

"Well, come on. I don't have all day."

Jackie flushed, but she adjusted her dress and held out her hand. "I'm Jackie. Lisa's sister."

Dee looked at her hand and rolled her eyes. "A hundred for fifteen minutes and all we do is talk. Unless . . ." She tried to look around Jackie to see if I was aroused. "Unless you want more."

"No touching is fine. I just want to find out about my

sister." Jackie dug into her purse.

"Come with me," Dee said.

She led us into her bedroom. There was one recliner chair and a king-size bed.

"I'll be right back," Dee said, taking Jackie's money.

Jackie pressed back against me and rubbed her sweet ass against my erection. "Maybe we should get a room. Not here," she amended. "Once we get the information, we could find a cheap hourly hotel and then go at it like bunnies."

I held her close because I liked the feel of her body. "You know you're only wearing a skimpy dress," I murmured in her ear. She shivered against me. "I could just flip it up and start fucking you now. I'll give Dee another hundred to fuck off for another fifteen minutes."

"No," she said. "Not here."

I sat on the recliner and pulled her onto my lap again. My hand slipped under her dress.

"Miles," Jackie said, breathlessly. "She'll be back any minute."

"Then you better come quickly. Because I don't want to fuck you in a cheap no-tell hotel. We're going to out to dinner and a show, and then we'll spend the rest of the night in my bed. After a rousing bout of morning sex, we're going to go out for breakfast. And then, we'll deal with Lisa's shit."

"That sounds like a plan." She smiled and it made my head spin.

"Granny panties again?" I sighed, but I was delighted, especially when she spread her legs wider so I could get easier access. She was already wet. "You're lucky I don't have condoms with me. I'd already be inside you."

"Um," she said, clutching my shoulders and closing her eyes when my fingers sank into her wet heat. "What if we get caught?"

"Do you think you're going to embarrass the hooker?" I

hoped Dee would take her time because I owed Jackie a great orgasm. I tickled my fingers through her, deeper until I found her clit. I rubbed it with my knuckle back and forth.

Jackie sucked in her breath and touched her forehead with mine. "That feels so good." Her fingers tangled in my hair as she held my head to hers. She clamped her legs together, and I rubbed faster.

"Miles," she whispered, her eyes wild and frantic. "Hurry."

"Just this once." I kissed her.

Grinding down on my hand, Jackie started to shake apart. She screamed into my mouth and went limp. I reluctantly slid my fingers out of her and adjusted her panties. I slowly licked my fingers clean while she watched me with hooded eyes.

The door opened and Jackie jumped off my lap. I needed a few moments to get myself under control.

"Where's my sister?" Jackie said before Dee could get a word out. Good idea, leading with an offense.

"Carson City. She's doing wine tasting tours at Paloma Vineyards."

Jackie looked back at me, but I was already on my phone checking the place out. "She got that job after leaving here two weeks ago?"

Dee nodded.

"And she's still there?"

"As far as I know."

"Why couldn't you tell us this over the phone?" I asked.

"Because you went to my mom. That's a bullshit thing to do. So I figured I owed you." Dee flounced on the bed. "Besides, it's nice to get a paid break during my shift."

"Why did she come here to Pahrump?" Jackie asked, cutting me off from bitching Dee out further.

"To piss Parker off and make him chase her."

"Who exactly is Parker?" Jackie asked.

"He was her regular at Dalton's."

The mysterious white haired dude. Finally, we were getting somewhere.

"None of the other girls could get close to him but Lisa," Dee continued. "Turns out, he's a producer and she wanted to get into a musical that he's going to do in Carson City. He was in Vegas raising funds for it and she offered to become a partner. But as a bartender, she wasn't making enough money."

Jackie shot me another look and I nodded. Now we knew why she became a stripper. I Googled "Parker producer," but I wasn't getting anything helpful.

"Zeke had set me up in Pahrump in an apartment a long time ago. I would entertain his friends when he needed me to and in return I could stay there and freelance when I wasn't working in Dalton's."

"Zeke is your pimp," I said bluntly.

"*Was* my pimp. Now I'm a free agent." She looked around the room. "Sort of. It's complicated. Anyway while Lisa was still at Dalton's, she bitched to me that she needed more money in order to finance Parker's show. I had the apartment in Pahrump. I figured she could try her hand at escorting. But she's too uptight. So she decided to do exotic dancing at Dalton's instead of bartending. Well, Parker nearly lost his mind. He bought up all of her dances and I think he really fell for her. But he told her that he'd never date a stripper."

While Jackie was digesting that, I had questions of my own.

"Why did you, Zeke, and Paulie quit at the same time?" I asked.

"I quit because I got the job here. You have to stay on the property for the length of your contract so I couldn't drive to Vegas to make my shift at Dalton's." She looked down at her hands. "I didn't give notice because Liu is a shitheel and I had to start here immediately. I don't know about Zeke and Paulie. As far as I know, they're still working at Dalton's."

"They're not," I said.

"Back to Lisa," Jackie butted in. "How did she end up in Pahrump if she didn't want to go from being a stripper to a hooker?"

"Escort," Dee corrected.

Jackie made an impatient gesture with her hand. "Whatever. Sex for money. When she left her Vegas apartment. She said she had room and board."

"She did. I let Lisa stay with me. Zeke didn't care as long as I kept escorting his friends. Lisa got the job here and would work while I was entertaining in the apartment."

"What about Parker? He's her boyfriend now, isn't he?"

"He is now. When he went to Dalton's one night and found out she vanished without a trace, he freaked out."

"I know the feeling," Jackie said dryly.

"She knew how to play him. She told Zeke to casually let it slip to Parker that Lisa was now working at a chicken ranch. Parker came riding in to rescue her, only to find out she was bartending instead of prostituting." Dee snickered. "Anyway, Parker was fine with her being a bartender. So they started dating, but money was still a problem. She just wasn't making bank like the rest of us. It pissed her off. I know Parker didn't like her working at a house of ill repute even if she wasn't selling her ass. I think she's living with him now, but I'm not sure. She doesn't return my calls."

"Join the club," Jackie said. "I think we're done here."

I got up. "I've got a few more questions."

"You've got the time," Dee said. She knew me better than to offer me anything else and I appreciated her not trying to hustle me to pay for a sex act with her. "What about Cordon Bleu?"

She brightened up. "I'm still going to go. This time to Paris. As soon as I make enough money." Dee's face dimmed a little. "It can't come soon enough."

"Did Zeke stay with you in the apartment?"

"Not usually. We have a business relationship. I don't see him that way. Of course, the son of a bitch came here on my first shift. It was easy money, but that was the only way I'd sleep with him and he knew it."

"Did you ever see him or Paulie do drugs?"

"Yeah, we all did some. It wasn't a big deal."

"Were you selling out of the club?"

"We weren't. Ginny was the only one who was into that." She dropped that like it was a big reveal.

"Leonidas supplied her, right?" I asked casually, playing a hunch.

"Probably." Dee said. "The Rivs are getting more into the local businesses. I figured you were okay with it."

I held on to my temper. "What do you know about the Rivs?"

"Zeke would know more. He brought them to me a few times."

"Leonidas?"

"Once or twice, but mostly his lieutenants. They brag and talk."

"Was Paulie selling?"

"No, but he talked a good game. He's in love with Ginny. I think he pretended to sell to make himself look cool." Dee rolled her eyes.

Grier might be able to get something helpful out of Dee. I'd have to suggest that he come up here to "talk" with her. "I'm sorry Liu was such a prick to you. You could have come to me and I would have ended it."

"I was going to leave anyway as soon as one of the brothels picked me up. I was more sick of not being able to negotiate my own prices when Zeke set me up with dates."

"Is the security tight here?"

She nodded. "They're always on top of things. If you're

ever looking for a job, I'll put in a good word for you."

Jackie grabbed my hand and tugged. "He won't be. We'll leave you to it. If Lisa calls you, can you tell her to call me?"

"Sure," Dee said. "And Miles, come back anytime."

Ugh. She had to go there.

Jackie pulled me out of the room and didn't say a word to me until we were in the car.

"Did you think Angelique was pretty?"

I shrugged. "I guess. The feathers were a bit distracting. You're prettier."

She smiled, linking her fingers through mine. I started the car and headed back to Vegas.

"I know we had plans tonight. Can we alter them?" Jackie asked.

I hid a sigh. "Of course."

"How long is it to Carson City?"

"By car, about six hours. If you charter a plane, it's about an hour. If you go the regular airport route, it's cheaper but by the time you're past security it's about double that time."

"You know I've got to go to Carson City, right?"

"Yeah," I said slowly. I knew where this was going.

"How about you come with me? We'll get dinner at the airport and skip the show. We'll land too late for the winery to be open, but I figure we could have our evening in my hotel room in Carson City. The rest of the plan can stay the same."

She surprised me. I'd figured she'd want to storm the winery.

"Sounds like a great plan. I especially like the part where the next day you confront Lisa and then get back to enjoying your vacation."

"Me too. Okay. You drive us back to the Wynn and I'll make all the arrangements."

Jackie already had her phone out.

CHAPTER SIXTEEN

Jackie Mitchell

I was spending a lot more money than I had originally planned on. Yeah, I was sticking it to Lisa by staying at the Wynn, but the plane tickets and the bribes/tips I'd been paying out were starting to add up. I didn't want to bankrupt Lisa, if she was even going to be able to pay me back from any residuals or royalties she was still getting from the odd commercial or television show. While my mother would probably cover anything Lisa couldn't, she shouldn't have to. This could have all been solved by a few simple phone calls.

I understood now why Lisa had been so vague and hadn't bothered to explain things to Mom. She had been ping-ponging all over Nevada doing one sketchy job after another. And this Parker dude could be stringing her along as well. If she was struggling so hard to finance Parker's play, I was hoping it wasn't a scam and that she hadn't already given him her life savings. I hated when my mother was right. Lisa did need someone to watch out for her.

Miles had gone back to Dalton's while I packed an overnight bag. He had a bunch of things to take care of and was on the phone for most of the drive back from Pahrump. I felt a little guilty about taking him away from his job, but his support was the only thing keeping me centered. My emotions were flying all over the place. I was running out of spending cash, but the end was in sight.

Placing a hand on my stomach to calm the jumpiness I felt, I took some deep breaths. All I had to do was make it until tomorrow. I'd talk to Lisa at the winery, report back to Mom, and I would still have a few days in Vegas with Miles. And if I were lucky, my family would leave me alone to enjoy it. I'd never been to the Hoover Dam or the Grand Canyon and I was hoping Miles could take some time off from work and do some touristy things with me.

I didn't know why I was so nervous. Things were looking up.

"You haven't found her yet," I said to my reflection as I paused to see if I looked as disheveled as I felt. She better be at this winery and that bitch Dee better not have tipped her off that we were coming.

Luckily, the chartered flight saved us time at the airport. It was costly, about a hundred and fifty dollars each way, but we were there in an hour and ten minutes. I didn't even have time to suggest to Miles that we join the mile-high club.

We checked into the Carson City hotel, which was more of a budget-type place than the Wynn. But it was clean, and it had a soft bed. By the time we were settled, the winery had long since closed. I was glad. I wasn't up for a confrontation with Lisa right now.

"You're tense," Miles said, coming up behind me as I looked out into the parking lot from the hotel's window. His big hands landed on my shoulders and when he started to massage them, I let out a deep, appreciative sigh.

"It's been a long week," I said. The view wasn't as nice as the one outside of the Wynn.

"Any regrets?" he asked.

I turned so I was in the circle of his arms. "Not one."

The hotel room may have been a little shabby, but it all faded away when his mouth touched mine. *Finally*. Finally, we were alone and had all the time in the world to explore each other. I kicked off my shoes as he pulled my shirt over my head.

"Disappointed there're no angel wings?" I said breathlessly.

"Not at all. You better be wearing your granny panties."

I slithered out of my shirt and stood there in my all-white cotton bra and underwear.

Miles groaned. "You're so sexy."

"Dalton's has warped you," I said.

"In more way than one," he agreed.

"Your turn."

He tossed off his shirt and stepped out of his shoes while I took off his belt and pants.

"I should have made you do a striptease for me." I held him tight, shamelessly running my hands over his muscled back and tight ass.

"I'm no dancer." Miles pulled my hair away from my neck and made me go up on my toes with the slight scrape of his five o'clock shadow on my sensitive spots.

"You're a tough guy. Surely, you know karate patterns or something."

"That's not sexy."

"Oh, speak for yourself. All those rippling muscles." I tugged down his boxers and would have eagerly taken him in my mouth, but he stopped me by threading his fingers through my hair and tugging me up.

"That gets me hot," I told him.

"I know." He trailed his hand down to my ass. "You've been frustrating me lately. I've been wanting to give this a few hard smacks."

He demonstrated.

I wiggled against him. "Not my kink unless you're balls deep inside me. Then you can paddle my ass and I'll probably come all over your cock."

"Fuck," he groaned. "Give me that dirty little mouth."

Hot and hard, his lips tangled with mine as he backed me toward the bed. I sank back into the soft, clean linens and pulled him with me. Miles was one step ahead of me, kissing down to my belly and gently sliding my underwear off my legs.

Starting at my ankle, he kissed and nibbled up my thigh. I shrieked and tried to get away, but not seriously. I wanted to feel his heavy body on top of me, instead of the tickling teasing. But then he got to the juncture of my thighs. He shot me a wicked grin and then he was kissing me down there just as passionately as he had my mouth. With both of my thighs on his shoulders, I was at the mercy of the sweet swipes of his tongue. My hips rose and fell in rhythm to his fast licks.

"Miles," I moaned, gripping the covers. Staring up at the cracked ceiling, I listened to the wet sounds his mouth made as he probed deeper into me. "Fuck," I whispered when his tongue swiped over my clit. I lost the use of language when his lips clamped around it and sucked. My thighs tightened around his cheeks and I knew I'd have razor burn on my inner thighs in the morning, but I didn't care.

My body clenched and I came, shivering, bucking, and making animal noises.

"That's what I like," he murmured, kissing back up my body. Pulling my bra up, Miles didn't bother to even take it off. His mouth sucked in one nipple, while his hand cupped and fondled my other breast.

"I want you between my thighs," I muttered, trying to rid myself of the tangled bra. I could feel his hot cock, velvety soft but rock hard against my hip.

"Right here?" Miles lifted his head from my reddened nipple as his fingers left my breast and trailed down my body. He plunged two fingers inside me, fucking me with them while he kissed me deep.

Pulling his hair so he would stop kissing me, I said. "Please. Fuck me."

"Come again and I will." Leaning over, he took my other nipple into his mouth and sucked hard.

Gritting my teeth in sweet frustration, I met each thrust of his fingers. "Miles, I want you. Please." I gasped as his fingers brought me close to the edge.

His mouth on my throat again, Miles moved back to my tortured clit and rubbed it just like I liked. My mind flashed back to the brothel where he had easily made me come all over his hand. The thrill of almost getting caught, of being in such a naughty place, put a smile on my face. New York Jackie would never had done such a thing.

I sighed and held Miles tight. Kissing me, he alternated between thrusting his fingers inside me and tickling my clit. Each little stroke sent frissons of desire through me.

"Miles now," I begged, lifting my knee so I could stretch my leg over my head.

"Fuck," he said and fumbled back. "I need a condom."

I held my leg in place, and I played with myself while he dove for his overnight bag and juggled the box of condoms back to bed. I loved looking at him. Naked, he was all muscles and tattoos and I couldn't wait to have his thick hard cock back inside me.

"Please," I said when he just looked at me.

"You didn't come," he said. "Let me see you come, beautiful,"

That was easy. My fingers knew just what to do as I stared at him. "Oh," I cried out as the orgasm snuck up on me, crashing pleasure over pleasure through me.

Miles dove inside, riding the wave with me. I wrapped my legs around his waist and hung on. The bed creaked fast and the headboard slammed hard against the wall. I hoped the people in the next room were listening and getting turned on. I laughed, but it turned into a deep satisfied moan.

"Harder," I panted, loving the slapping sounds our bodies made in addition to the bedsprings and the hammering against the wall. Miles's fingers dug into the mattress on either side of my head. His eyes were wild, his lips pulled back into a feral snarl of pleasure. He pummeled me back into the mattress, each thrust thick and deep. I bit his shoulder and he swore. Sealing his mouth over mine, he kissed me until I screamed inside his mouth as everything narrowed down to the feeling of his body pumping into mine. When I closed my eyes, lights flashed under my eyelids. Every sensation was highlighted, from the scrape of my tender nipples on his raspy chest hair, to the taste of myself on his tongue, I was in sensory overload.

Miles rolled us over and steadied me when I would have fallen off him. He nearly slipped out and I sat up quickly so as not to lose him. He gripped my hips, so I felt his full length. We stared at each other, breathing heavily.

"I've been wanting you on my cock like this since your little lap dance in Dalton's."

I lifted myself up and down slowly. Miles hissed in plea-sure. I dragged my nails down his chest, not hard enough to leave a mark, but hard enough for him to know I meant busi-ness. He slapped my ass then and my entire body shook.

"Dance," he said hoarsely.

"There's no music."

He swatted me again. I liked the burn when I was

stretched on top of him like this. I began to move, using his body to come. Winding my arms over my head, I stretched and bounced. Panting, I had to lean down and hold his shoulders to get the angle I needed. It made my breasts brush his face.

Miles held them close so he could lick and suck on both nipples at once. I held on and rocked to the beat of the headboard and danced to the screech of the bedsprings. Harder and harder I danced on him. I came apart, clutching half-moons into his chest and crying out his name.

He pushed me gently and I landed on my back, still trying to catch my breath. Flipping me over, Miles yanked me to all fours and plunged back into me again.

"Yes," I groaned over and over again. He tangled his fingers in my hair and pulled. I went wild but he held me there, fucking me from behind, his own breathing now ragged grunts. I lost count of how many times he made me come, but the pounding of his hips grew frantic. Miles clutched me tight and snarled a guttural curse as he jerked and came.

I was boneless. I accepted his heavy weight and never wanted to move again.

"Jackie," he said after several long minutes and a few attempts to speak.

"Mmmm," I said, already half asleep.

"I never want to let you go."

I smiled. I felt the same way.

CHAPTER SEVENTEEN

Miles Carvello

My phone was ringing. I let it go to voice mail. Jackie was zonked out over my chest and I was spent from the wild love-making. When it rang again, I knew it was trouble. Carefully easing out from under her, I grabbed my phone and took it into the bathroom and closed the door. I wasn't surprised that it was Highway calling. I was surprised that it was only two in the morning. Seemed like it should be later.

"What, for fuck's sake?" I said.

"Ginny's here."

"She's late."

"Thought you'd like to know."

"Keep an eye on her." I had told Highway that I'd changed my mind about Ginny and decided to give her a second chance. It made him suspicious because I never gave anyone a second chance. "Was that all?" I wanted to get back to Jackie and feel her lithe body against me. I was starting to get my second wind.

"Paulie's back too."

"Shit." I wanted to talk to him about the bullshit drugs and the gun.

"Do you want me to have a few words with him?"

"No. Don't scare him off. Zeke's not there too, is he?"

"No."

"Does Paulie seem frantic, like there was something missing from his locker?"

"Not that I heard."

"Check around."

"We got a thief?"

"I don't know what we got. How's security looking?"

"A few drunks. One guy tried licking Raven."

I winced. "Was there anything left of him by the time you got there?"

"Plenty, and I learned a few new Russian curse words."

"It's good to have a hobby. Has anyone approached Ginny for anything other than a lap dance?"

"Nope."

"If she goes back into the dressing room with someone, let it happen."

"Are you getting a cut of the action now? Is that why she's back?" Highway's tone was flat with disapproval.

"No, but trust me on this. I've got it covered."

"How long are you going to be playing house in Carson City?"

"I'll be back tomorrow before prime time. Don't get your panties in a bunch."

"I go commando."

"And I needed to know that why?"

"Something sweet to think about before drifting off to sleep."

I shook my head. "I'm going to bed. Don't call me unless the club is on fire or you run into something you can't handle. Everything else can wait until tomorrow night."

"You got it, boss."

I turned my phone off for the first time in two years. Dalton's could get along without me for a day. I hoped.

The next morning I convinced Jackie to take a shower with me. I loved the feel of her soapy breasts in my hands. And she loved rubbing my cock, slicked up with the same slippery suds.

"I'm going to come in your hands." I lifted my mouth from hers to tell her.

"Yes," she breathed, arching into me. "You are."

"I don't want to stop fondling these to flick you into an orgasm."

"I'm a little sore this morning," she admitted, ducking her head shyly.

"Sorry about that."

"No, I enjoyed it." Jackie rubbed me harder.

Closing my eyes, I enjoyed her hard caress. "Why don't you give me a lap dance on my face then?"

"Not until you shave." She gasped when I slammed both hands onto the wall to keep my balance.

I came all over her soapy hands and let the hot spray of the shower rinse us clean.

"I'll go shave." I kissed her again.

"You're going to drown me." She laughed.

Staggering out of the shower, I thought it was funny that I was a little weak in the knees. I must be getting old if marathon sex was slowing me down. I toweled off and wrapped it around my waist. I had just finished shaving when Jackie stepped out of the shower.

"You all right?" I asked as she steadied herself on my shoulder. "I was about to send out a search party.

Jackie wrapped her arms around me and laid a cheek

against my back. "Just enjoying a long hot shower. I'm usually in the office and have had several client meetings by now." She yawned. "Let's go hit a buffet or something. I could eat my shoes, I'm so hungry."

"We can go to the Carson City Casino. They've got an all-you-can-eat spread that I hear is pretty decent."

"I guess I have to get dressed," she said grumpily.

"We could get room service," I suggested. "Unless you're still sore."

"I should be okay by lunch." She reached around and untucked my towel.

"I'm sorry I was so rough," I said, feeling a little guilty.

Jackie poked her head from around my body and smiled at me in the mirror. "It's not you. I'm not used to all this dancing and fucking. But I'm getting there."

"Good."

The breakfast buffet was a work of art. I had steak and eggs and a side of hash browns. I was considering going up and getting an omelet when Jackie's phone rang.

"I don't recognize the number," she said, "But it could be Lisa."

"You better take it. I'm going up for round two. Do you want something?"

"Chocolate croissant."

I nodded and left to fill my plate. When I got back, our coffees had been refilled, but Jackie had her head in her hands.

"Did something happen?" I asked as a wave of alarm when through me.

She lifted her head. Her eyes were brimming over with tears. I snatched her hand and rubbed it. Then I noticed she was grinning like a fool.

"*Travesty* called me back. They narrowed down to five people and I'm one of the five."

"That's fantastic. When do they want to see you?"

"Tonight. Apparently, one of the backers is flying in and wants a say in the casting. It's at seven p.m. We should be back by then, right?"

"Plenty of time. But we should finish up here so we're there when the winery opens."

"Good idea." Jackie got up to leave, but I tugged her down.

"We've got time to finish your coffee and chocolate croissant."

"Right," she said. "I'm still reeling. I never thought I'd make it this far. They actually called me back. Thank goodness I was able to sub in my information for Lisa's. That way Zimmerman never has to know."

"Unless you get the job."

Jackie shook her head. "I can't think about that now. One step at a time. If I start making plans, and it doesn't happen, I'll be crushed."

I felt a flicker of satisfaction that she was considering taking the job. I wouldn't push now, but I was going to make it very easy for her to say yes to staying in Las Vegas with me.

"It will be good to see Lisa and talk to her," Jackie said, cupping her coffee mug in her hands.

"Are you sure she'll want to see you?"

"Probably not," Jackie said. "But ask me if I give a fuck."

That's my girl.

The drive out to the winery was uneventful and we were the first ones in for the tour. Jackie immediately went into the bar area and I followed. It was a tourist trap, with wine barrel tables and fussy chairs. I wasn't much for wine. I just wanted this over as quickly as possible so Jackie could concentrate on her second audition.

"Is Lisa Mitchell working today?" Jackie asked one of the

bartenders, who had a set of wine glasses in front of her and several open bottles.

"No, she quit last week."

"What?"

The woman flinched at Jackie's vehemence.

"Sorry," Jackie apologized. "It's just that I've come all the way from New York to see her and she mentioned that she was working here."

"Yeah, that sounds like Lisa. She's only interested in one person, herself."

Jackie opened her mouth to argue, but then switched gears. "Parker isn't here is he?"

"Parker who?"

"Her boyfriend?"

"I didn't know she had a boyfriend," the bartender said. "But maybe that's why she left without giving notice. She seemed the type to let a man call the shots for her."

I could see Jackie's shoulders slumping and I stepped in closer for moral support.

"You don't happen to know where she went or why she left?" Jackie asked, slinging an arm around me. I gave her a quick hug.

"She said she got a new job, but she didn't tell us where."

Jackie sighed and dug into her handbag for her card. "I'm her sister. Is there any way you can give me the address she put down on her application? I need to find her. Our mother is terribly worried about her."

"I'm sorry. I can't."

"What about the owner or the manager?"

"I *am* the owner."

"I can prove that I'm her sister."

"I can't divulge personal information. I could get in trouble."

"She's right," I said, when Jackie would have protested

more. I'd bent the rules and it was only because Grier owed me a few favors that he did the background check on Jackie that made me comfortable giving out Lisa's address.

"Was Lisa all right? She has a bad knee."

"Seemed fine to me."

"Do you have any idea where I could start looking for her?" Jackie said, in a small voice. "Like I said, I came all this way."

"Why don't you call her?" the bartender owner asked.

"She doesn't answer or call me back."

"Take a hint," the bartender said, not unkindly. "Now, would you like to sample some of our wines?"

"No thanks," I said and steered Jackie back to the rental car I'd sprung for. It beat waiting on a car service or taxi and I was glad for the privacy as I helped her into the passenger seat.

She waited until I closed the door before wailing, "What do I do now?"

"I don't know, sweetheart."

"She could be anywhere. Hell, for all I know, if she's no longer with Parker she could be heading back to New York."

"Maybe that's what happened," I said, stroking her hair.

"No, I'm not that lucky."

"She's a selfish bitch," I said and was surprised when Jackie flinched. "What?"

"There's got to be a reason why she keeps taking these jobs and then leaving after a few days or weeks."

"Perhaps she's trying to find herself," I said sarcastically, but Jackie was nodding her head.

"I think so too. Don't get me wrong, I think she's going about it the wrong way. But you've seen what our mother is like. I think she doesn't want to call until she's settled. My mother has a way of shitting all over new plans and dreams."

"She gets more and more delightful the more I hear about her."

"Lisa's always accused me of being her stooge. I wish I had handled things better in the past so that she would trust me now. It kills me that she trusts Parker more than her family and I don't have a good feeling about him."

"That's New York Jackie talking," I said, smiling when she looked up at me in surprise. "New York Jackie lets Lisa and her mother walk all over her."

"Not always," she said defensively.

"Las Vegas Jackie was getting more independent. Look, we're out of clues and I know you're out of patience. Let's get back to Las Vegas and get you ready for your second interview."

She gave me a small smile. "It seems so unimportant in the grand scheme of finding my sister."

"Lisa doesn't want to be found. I don't see how this changes your plans. You've done all you can. The trail is stone cold."

"At least her leg seems to be holding up."

"And she's not a prostitute or an exotic dancer. Not that there's anything wrong with either of those professions," I said.

Jackie nodded. "I don't know what to tell my mother."

"Tell her the truth. You tracked her to a winery in Carson City, but she quit that job, and no one knows where she went. If your mother wants to know more, than she can hire a private detective. You have a life to get back to."

"I just wish we could find this Parker person. We might have to go back to Pahrump and see if anyone knows more."

I did not want to go back to the brothel, but I'd cross that bridge when we came to it. "Let's just go home."

"Home," Jackie huffed. "I'm not even sure where that is anymore."

After checking out of the motel, we headed to the chartered plane. They were able to schedule us for a return flight back to Vegas sooner than we had originally requested. As we were about to board the plane, though, Jackie stopped dead in her tracks.

"What?"

She was staring at a poster that was tacked up to a support pole. I went over and looked. It was advertising a new burlesque review. There was a large martini glass and a picture of Jackie's sister sitting inside it. She wore long black gloves and was hanging over the rim of the glass suggestively. Opening night was tonight.

At seven p.m.

"You can't," I said.

"I can't risk losing her again," Jackie said. "I know she'll be performing here tonight." She ripped down the poster and folded it into her purse. "I'm sorry. You can go back without me."

I pretty much had to. I had a lot of shit going down at the bar. I wanted to talk to Paulie and Ginny as soon as possible.

"How long is the show running for?" I asked.

"It didn't say on the poster."

"Call up the box office and find out."

"Why?"

"Because you can damn well put yourself first for once. Let's go and get you to your audition and we can come back tomorrow."

Jackie bit her lip. "I can't."

"You can."

"I'm going to lose her again."

"Let me see that poster?"

She frowned. "Why?"

"Please?"

Jackie handed it to me as if she was afraid I would tear it

up. Scanning it, I pointed out a name. "Parker Templeton, producer."

She let out a shaky breath.

"We found Parker. If Lisa bolts, we'll be right behind her. But I don't think she will. She's got the guy. She's got the show. Where else is she going to go?"

"Is there a problem?" the flight attendant called from the portable stairs leading up to the plane. "We need to be wheels up in five."

"On our way," I said.

"I shouldn't," she said.

"You should. It's one day."

"I should be there for her opening night."

"No. She knows you're in Nevada. If she wanted you there, she would have called."

"Do you think she's going to go full nude and she's embarrassed? Maybe that's why she didn't call."

I stared at the flyer again. "Nope, they're serving alcohol. Two-drink minimum."

"That sounds familiar."

"Wine only. From Carson City Wineries."

"The owner lied to us."

Miles shrugged. "She might not have known. Maybe Lisa worked there to find out how to get a good price out of her or was hoping for an employee discount."

"That would explain why she didn't know who Parker was. He couldn't very well admit he'd sent in a spy." Jackie rubbed her forehead.

I put my arm around her and hustled her toward the plane. "We'll come back tomorrow."

"This is getting really expensive, this back and forth. I should save the money and just stay here. It's not like I'm going to leave New York to become a showgirl."

Her words hit me hard, but I didn't let her see it. I needed her to get into the plane. "That's beside the point. You wanted to know if you could do it. This could be your only chance."

Jackie sucked in a deep breath. "You're right."

I let out the sigh I was holding as she entered the plane and strapped in.

"You'll come with me tomorrow, right?" she asked as we taxied down the runway.

"No," I said. "I've got a bar to run."

"Oh," she said in a small voice and turned to the window.

I didn't give a shit about her selfish bitch of a sister and I had no desire to see Jackie and Lisa get into it. A part of me wanted to go for moral support and to soothe any hurt that Lisa could cause. But I needed to start distancing myself instead of deluding myself. Jackie wasn't going to leave her family or New York. Certainly not for a guy who owned a titty bar or a small part in an off-strip casino show. Who was I kidding? Jackie could dance on Broadway and fulfill her dream. I was just a vacation fling. Vacation flings didn't get involved in messy family situations.

I looked over at Jackie to see if she wanted to talk more. But her eyes were closed.

I guessed that was for the best.

CHAPTER EIGHTEEN

Jackie Mitchell

I sat on my bed in the Wynn trying not to hyperventilate. My audition was still several hours away. My mind was going a mile a minute. I was worried that Lisa was going to slip away and disappear. I was hurt that Miles wasn't going to go back to Carson City with me tomorrow. Although I didn't really blame him. I had taken enough of his time with the wild goose chase Lisa had led us all on.

I almost didn't answer it when my phone rang, but I saw it was Chance.

"Howzit?" he asked.

And suddenly I had a plan. "What are you and the boys doing tonight?"

"Are you on the pole this evening?" he asked.

"No," I said. "I've actually got a callback to audition tonight for a dancing part in the Odyssey casino's new show, *Travesty.*"

"Congrats. You'll blow them all the way. I can't wait to tell all the blokes that I knew you when."

Could you become a big star when you started out as a showgirl? Why not? I closed my eyes. Too much pressure. *I will not puke. I will not puke.*

"You all right?"

"Can you do me a favor? It's a big one."

"Go ahead."

"Miles and I tracked Lisa down."

"That's great news. But you don't sound so happy. What's the bad news?"

"Tonight is her opening night. She's the star of a burlesque show in Carson City. I can't be there because of my audition. I'm afraid she's going to rabbit, and I won't be able to pick up her trail again."

"What can I do?" Chance asked.

"It's an hour away by plane and it's about three hundred dollars round trip. I can pay your ticket. Do you think you could go to the show and talk to her afterward? She's had a crush on you forever. I know if you ask her to call me, she won't be able to refuse you."

"You're putting a lot of faith in a man she's never met."

"You were half naked on her wall for over a year. Just give her that cocky grin and she'll be putty in your hands."

"Give me the deets," he said.

I read him everything from the poster I had. "Can you come to the Wynn and I'll give you the money?"

"Don't worry your pretty little head about it. Three hundred dollars is a steak dinner to these arseholes. They'd love to fly on a charter plane to a burlesque show. And I for one, want to see who's the better dancer, you or Lisa."

"She is," I mumbled.

"She was," he said. "It's your turn to shine. I want to hear all about your audition. Just remember, you've got me and Miles in your corner."

"Yeah, I do. None of this would have happened if it weren't for Miles." I owed him big. After I got home from the audition, I'd go over to Dalton's and tell him that. And convince him to go back to the Wynn with me. I gave a test bounce on the bed. Not even the slightest squeak. That was all right—there were other noises to make.

"Chance, you're the greatest."

"I am, aren't I?"

"And so modest. Thank you so much for doing this for me." I owed Chance big too, but he was going to have to settle for a fruit basket or something.

"Like I said, we responsible siblings have to look out for each other."

"True. Have fun tonight."

"I think we will. I'll call you after."

I thanked him again and hung up.

Getting ready for the second callback was more nerve-racking than going to the first one. I had more time to plan and rehearse the number over and over again in my hotel room. I did my best thinking while I was dancing, but today my mind refused to settle down.

If I didn't get the job, no harm, no foul. The Zimmerman Agency would never have to know that I went instead of Lisa. If I did get the job—my feet tripped up and I used the bed to catch my fall.

"Nice one, Jackie," I said to myself. "Be sure to do that on stage. That will really impress them."

I forced myself to sit still while I finished the thought. If I did get the job, I would have to turn it down and I would have wasted the casting director's and the producer's time. Or I would have to reroute my entire life and move from New York to Nevada. On the plus side, I was pretty sure Miles would let me stay with him until I found a place out here. On the negative side, it was going to be expensive —even if I got someone to sublet my apartment until my lease ran out. I was almost out of the thousand dollars my mother had floated me this week, and that was earmarked for Lisa's search and rescue anyway. It was nonsense. Ridiculous.

And yet I felt giddy and happy like a kid on Christmas Eve.

"Don't get your hopes up," I told myself.

But what if? a little voice in my head insisted. *Why not?*

Miles Carvello

Leonidas showed up with a couple of his soldiers that night. I couldn't risk them seeing Jackie, so I sent her a quick text telling her not to come to Dalton's tonight, but that I'd love to see her later if she wanted company. I was trying to get in as much time as I could before she left.

"They're looking to talk to you, boss," Highway said over the headset. "You want me to send them back to your office?"

"No, set them up with a round of beers on the house. I'll be right there."

I called Grier and left him a message to get his ass over here as fast as he could because I had Leonidas and the Rivs in the bar tonight, along with Ginny and Paulie, the patsy dishwasher. Among all of them, there might be something actionable. I just wanted Jackie far away from the action.

Walking out into the club, I saw Ginny was giving Leonidas a lap dance while the other three goons looked on. "Yellow alert," I muttered into my headset and the security team went to their positions. I hoped this was a peaceful visit, but I had a feeling it wasn't.

Taking a chair from a nearby table, I brought it over to Leonidas's table and positioned it so my back was to the stage. Kikki, who had just walked out to the pole, glared at me, but I ignored her. These guys wouldn't be throwing tips.

"You wanted to see me?" I said to Leonidas while Ginny writhed all over him.

"That's good enough, sweetheart." Leonidas gave Ginny's ass a sharp slap.

Ginny met my eyes. I raised my eyebrow. Did she want me to do something about it? She gave a slight shake of her head.

"Keep your hands to yourself," I said mildly instead of throwing him out.

"Ginny doesn't mind? Do you?"

"No, Leo. Not with you," she simpered and swayed away on her five-inch stilettos.

"Don't touch my dancers," I said again, just in case he was going to try that shit with any of the others.

"Relax. I didn't come here to cause problems."

"That's good. Why are you here then?" I nodded as the waitress handed me my club soda and lime. I did a double take. It was Zeke's sister. Liu must have hired her when I wasn't here. I'd have to make sure everything was in order with payroll. Or maybe I could let my people do their jobs. It was tough to let go of all of the responsibility, but I was getting there.

"We heard about your problem the other night with the gas leak."

"It was a prank."

"A costly one."

I grunted.

"We could stop things like that from happening."

"I told you two years ago I wasn't interested in protection." I eyed the other three gang members. One of them blanched and looked away. He was probably one of the ones I'd sent to the hospital.

"And you don't need it. Your reputation precedes you. But the utility companies don't give a damn if you're Europe's hottest floor man. We could have gotten you back in business within the hour."

I had to consciously unclench my jaw. "That would have been helpful." I was being shaken down, and this time it was because Leonidas had bribed people in public works. There wasn't much I could do about that. "How much is this insurance going to cost me?"

"Ten grand a month," Leonidas said pleasantly.

"Go fuck yourself," I said in the same tone.

The three goons went to stand up, but Leonidas waved them to sit back down again. "I actually like you, Miles. I liked your uncle too. No one here wants to see Dalton's go the way Uncle Johnny's did."

I saw Grier sit down at a nearby table and pay Ginny to give him a lap dance. He was close enough to hear the conversation and Ginny dancing on him was a good cover.

"That kind of cash would impact my profits enough that I'd close within a year. I don't have that many gas leaks called in to warrant paying the Rivs protection money." I didn't raise my voice, but I hoped Grier was getting this anyway.

"These pranks have a way of escalating," Leonidas said. "How did the fire start in Uncle Johnny's Gentlemen's Club?"

"It was faulty wiring," one of his goons said.

"I heard it wasn't up to code," another said.

"How's your wiring looking?" Leonidas asked with an air of innocence.

I was going to kill him. I had a moment to consider leaping across the table and banging that smug smile into the floor. The other three would be on my unprotected back with knives. I couldn't count on Grier to break cover and help me. A quick glance around the room told me that my security team would be a few seconds too late.

"Are you saying the Rivs could have stopped Uncle Johnny's from burning down?"

A shadow crossed Leonidas' face. "You're doubting my word?"

"I'm considering your offer. Did you give my uncle the same deal?"

"We weren't operating this street back then."

I hadn't thought so.

"Trouble," Highway said in my ear. I looked up and Jackie was coming straight for us. Shit. I didn't want her to be any part of this.

"Who was?" I said casually. "That information would be worth more to me than greasing bureaucrats."

I saw Mav step in front of Jackie and escort her back to the dressing room. One less thing to worry about.

"Five thousand up front and I'll give you the names of the people responsible."

"How do I know you'd give me the right people?"

Leonidas gave a nasty laugh. "They're trying to reclaim old territory. The Rivs aren't going to give it to them."

"I'm going to need proof that they did it."

"I can't give you a signed confession, but you should be able to beat one out of them. If you got rid of them, it would be doing us a favor."

I narrowed my eyes. "Shouldn't you be paying me, then?"

"It doesn't work that way," Leonidas said. "My cousin speaks very highly of you. If he hadn't . . . well, that's not even worth talking about. You bring me five thousand dollars and the Rivs will leave Dalton's alone. We won't help, but we won't trash the place. In return, you take the men who murdered your uncle and burned down his club and make them go away."

I hoped Grier was getting all of this. "I don't have the cash tonight, but I can get it for you by noon tomorrow."

"Noon is good enough." Leonidas nodded.

"If you gentlemen will excuse me then, I've got a club to run." I dragged the chair back and plopped it at Grier's table. He didn't look up from Kikki, and I walked back to the dressing room.

The five dancers were in various state of undress when I walked in. Ginny ambushed me with a hug before I could stop her.

"I knew you couldn't live without me." She missed kissing me because I ducked away.

"Knock it off," I growled.

Jackie leaned up against the wall with her arms crossed. She raised an eyebrow.

"What did Leonidas want?" Ginny asked.

"None of your fucking business. If you want to know so bad, go back and ask him. VIP room three is free." Shit. If she could do that, I could set Grier up in my office to listen in.

"Fine," she drawled. "Are you fucking the new girl?" Ginny pointed at Jackie. "Because rumor has it, you are."

"Yes," Jackie said, before I could say anything. "He's fantastic in bed, in case you were wondering."

"For fuck's sake," I groaned.

The other girls whooped it up, but Ginny's lips tightened, then she flounced out.

"Sorry about that," I said, jerking a thumb in Ginny's direction.

"She's a nosy bitch."

"And a nasty one too," Mina said, reapplying her lipstick in the mirror.

"So what am I doing back here? The security guy said you wanted me in the dressing room. I had all sorts of kinky ideas, but it's a pretty busy place."

"Don't let us stop you," Betty said. "I'd throw some tips to see Miles in action."

I pointed at the door. "You're supposed to be on stage."

"Do you want me to dance too?" Jackie batted her eyelashes at me. "I thought I wasn't working here anymore."

"You're not. There's some dangerous gang members in the bar tonight and I didn't want them to see that you're with me." I took her by the elbow and walked out the back door with her. "I sent you a text."

"My phone's dead. I forgot to charge it."

"I've got some serious shit going down right now. I can't have you here. You're a distraction." I rubbed my hands up and down her arms. "In a good way, but I need to keep my head on straight."

"That sounds pretty serious," she said. "I'm worried."

"Don't be. It'll all be all right." I pulled her tight against me in a hug. No one worried about me. It was kind of cute. I whispered in her ear. "My security team is top-notch and Grier is here. I need to know that you're safe at the Wynn tonight. I'll come by and join you later, if that's okay?"

"More than okay." She kissed me and I wanted to linger, but I didn't want to risk any of the Rivs seeing us together.

"Go straight to the Wynn and stay there."

"I don't care what time you get through, come to me."

I nodded. "How did the audition go?"

Jackie sagged against me. "There's too much. I'll tell you later."

"You can't keep me hanging," I said. "Thumbs-up or thumbs-down?"

Shaking her head, she walked down the stairs. "I'll tell you later." When she got to the sidewalk, she turned back to me.

"Thank you. I've had the best time of my life this week. But mostly I want to let you know how much it's meant to me that you helped me find Lisa."

"Why does this sound like goodbye?" I asked, my gut clenching.

"Not yet, it's not. But I don't know what's going to happen with Lisa tomorrow, so I wanted to make sure you knew how I felt."

I didn't want to do this in a back alley over bags of garbage that had been stewing in the hot sun. And I sure as shit didn't want to do this when I wasn't anywhere near her. But I had to know.

"Is that all you feel?" I asked hoarsely.

"I'll tell you later." She gave me a seductive smile and walked away.

"Highway, send a few guys around the corner and make sure Jackie gets in her car okay," I said over the Bluetooth.

"Got it."

Going back inside, I made sure the two guards on the dressing room door knew that no one but me and the dancers were allowed back there tonight.

"If anyone has a problem with that, they can come to me," I said.

The club was picking up. All three stages had dancers on them, each woman writhing to hard core electronica. Javi had a light show going on that was almost as entertaining at the girls. Leonidas wasn't in his seat, but the three goons were enjoying the show. I didn't see Grier. Checking my phone, I saw he hadn't called either.

I went back to my office for a bit of peace and quiet while I thought about what I was going to do next. Grier was lying on the couch with a porno mag covering his face. I locked the door. "You're taking a risk coming into my office during prime business hours."

Grier sat up and tossed the magazine on my desk. "With the light show and those gorgeous dancers, if anyone saw me get up, they'd assume I was taking a piss instead of coming in here."

"I'm surprised security allowed you to get this far." When this was all over, I'd have a word with them.

"They didn't see me either. And since you gave me the key, it's all good."

I flipped through the VIP rooms' channels on my headset, but I didn't hear anything but music. "I think Ginny and Leonidas are in room three, but I don't hear any chatter. Did you catch Leonidas shaking me down?"

"Are you willing to wear a wire tomorrow when you give him the money?"

I nodded. "What if he's lying about knowing who killed my uncle?"

"It could be he's hoping you'll be hotheaded enough that you'd off one of his rivals. But he didn't say kill the men responsible. He said get them out of the picture. For all he knows, you would turn them over to the police after you roughed them up."

"What do you need me to do?"

Grier thought about it. "You know Ginny's a spy for him, right?"

I thought briefly about Ginny's sudden interest that Jackie and I were together. I was glad that I'd sent Jackie back to the Wynn and she wouldn't be in danger. The last thing I wanted was for Jackie to get hurt if they thought they could use her against me. It should be all right. She was safe in her hotel room, and tomorrow she was flying again to Carson City. By the time she got back here tomorrow night, it would all be over. I hoped.

CHAPTER NINETEEN

Jackie Mitchell

Lisa called around midnight.

"Holy shit," I said. "You do have my number."

"If you had sent Chance fucking Bateman a month ago, I would have called you back."

I sighed. "Are you going to call Mom tomorrow?"

"Probably not."

"Are you all right?"

"Let's go down Mom's list. I haven't lost my phone. I haven't been kidnapped. I'm not strung out on pills or drinking myself to death. And I'm not coming back to New York. Ever. Does that about cover all your questions? You have no idea what the last three months have been like."

Since she'd decided to be a snide bitch, I felt obligated to reply in the same manner. "You're no longer a stripper. You're not a hooker, but it was a close call. You are taking pain medication for your knee, and you've been quitting jobs and leaving people in the lurch all over Nevada. How am I doing for facts?"

I could hear the trombones of the burlesque music in the background. Since Lisa didn't have a quick answer for me, I continued.

"So, no. You've only answered half of my questions. I've got a pressing one for you tonight and I'd like to see you tomorrow to get the rest of them answered. If I'm going to have to go back to New York and face the firing squad, I want to be prepared."

"What?" Lisa snapped.

"How much money did you pay Parker to get him to give you the lead?"

"I was the clear choice for the star of the show," she said coldly.

"Okay, I phrased that wrong. How much money did you pay Parker so he could put on the show and are you getting paid for your performances?"

"That's two questions."

I was going to put her through the wall. She was lucky she was six hours' driving distance away from me. "Answer one of them."

"None of your business," she said sweetly.

"I'm your manager."

"You *were* my manager in New York. I don't need one here in Nevada."

"Is Parker your manager?"

"He's my boyfriend."

"I'm still your sister. I came all this way to make sure you were all right."

Lisa groaned. "I'm only three years younger than you. I'm an adult. I don't need to ask anyone's permission to move to Nevada."

"No, but a few phone calls would have gone a long way to

letting us know that you were safe and healthy."

"At times I wasn't," Lisa said. "But I needed to do that on my own too, without Mom and you hovering all over me."

"I didn't want to come down here. Mom made me."

Lisa scoffed. "Made you? Did she threaten to ground you? If you stopped and looked at your life, you'd run away too."

That stung. It had hints of truth in it as well. We could rip into each other all we wanted, but that wouldn't solve anything. "I'm concerned about Parker. If you're not going to tell Mom about the burlesque show, I'm going to have to."

"Don't you fucking dare."

"Why? What's she going to do? Ground you?" I said in a snotty rendition of her voice.

Yeah, I wasn't helping the situation. But I had a lot of anger and frustration I wanted to take out on her for the shitty way she'd treated me. "One phone call. Was that too much to ask when you knew I was in town?"

"I didn't want you to fuck up my opening night."

It was like she punched me in the stomach. Now, it was my turn to recover in silence.

"Look, I've got another set to do. I promised Chance I'd call to let you know that I'm alive and well and I don't need anything. Go home, Jackie. I'm staying here."

"It would still ease my mind if I could see you tomorrow. Can I take you and Parker out to lunch or something?"

She sighed. "I don't know. Sure. I guess. If that's what it takes for you to leave me alone."

"That's what it's going to take," I said. I needed to see her and Parker so I could report back to my mother and get her off both our backs.

"Fine. Meet us at the Goldmine Diner on Main Street at noon." Lisa hung up before I could say anything else.

I ordered a cheesecake from room service. Not a slice of cheesecake. A whole cake. And you can damn well bet I was charging Lisa for it. Of course, my mother was going to wind up paying for it, so revenge wasn't that sweet. Luckily, the cheesecake was. I hoped Miles would show up so I didn't have to eat the entire thing, but he didn't. The rat.

I had almost given up on him. The last time I checked the clock it was three a.m. After I disposed of the cheese-cake evidence, I had put on my sexy stripper outfit, but the thong annoyed the shit out of me. I decided to just be naked. But then I got cold, so I put on the fluffy robe. I must have fallen asleep because the heavy knock on my door sent me into a panic. Leaping out of bed, I barely managed to not to smack into the wall before I got my bearings. Peering through the peephole, I saw Miles and my heart did a crazy little jiggle.

"Come on in," I said, and hid a yawn.

"I'm sorry I'm so late. A lot of shit was happening tonight."

"Did you call the police on the gang members?"

"Didn't need to." He locked the door behind him. "I don't want to talk about that right now."

Grabbing his hand and leading him to the bed, I slid out of the robe. "You're overdressed."

"Are you sure you're not too tired?" he asked with a slow smile.

"I'll sleep afterward."

"As long as it's not during."

Miles shed his clothes and got under the covers with me. We held each other tight for a moment.

"This is nice," he said, kissing my forehead.

I melted into him. It was more than nice. It was sheer bliss. Coiling myself around him, I slowly stroked his back, his arms, his hips, and leg. Mine. All mine. He returned the favor by kneading my shoulders and back. I groaned and leaned into the massage.

"That feels incredible." I sighed. My eyelids drooped. I should have had coffee with the cake.

"How did the audition go?"

"It was intense." I tried to hide a yawn, but it was no good. "They had us do combo after combo. I think I fucked up one of the routines, but so did everyone else. I did a solo and a few group numbers." I stroked the hair away from his face. "I even got to wear one of the preliminary costumes. Those shoulder rigs are heavy. I almost went ass over teakettle into the orchestra pit until I found my balance."

"I'll take you to the gym with me and we can lift some weights."

"I don't think I'm in your league." I trailed a finger over his biceps.

Miles lay on his back and pulled me half on top of him. Straddling his leg, I fondled his cock.

"Mmm, I waited all day to have your hand there," he said sleepily.

Nuzzling his throat, I whispered, "Just my hand?"

"There wasn't a lot of time for fantasies." Tilting my head back, he kissed me softly. Miles felt like velvet steel in my hand as he hardened under my languorous strokes.

"I want to taste you, but I don't want you to stop."

I was already wet before he said that. Now I had a deep desire to feel his tongue in me. "That's easy enough," I said, switching positions.

Rolling all the way on top of him, I shrieked when he pulled my thighs to his mouth. My breasts brushed the hard plane of his abs. Stretching my hand out, I played with the silky hairs of his leg while I casually continued to stroke him with my other hand.

Miles kissed my pussy and gave it a long, slow lick. I shimmied closer. He held to his mouth, his powerful arms wrapped around my waist. I realized I was trapped when he found my clit and darted his tongue all around it. Sharp stabs of pleasure made me shake and writhe. I wiggled and ground against his face as he relentlessly pushed me closer to the edge. I had been so caught up in my desire that I was just holding him in my fist.

Taking him into my mouth, I sucked him deep and bobbed my head up and down his hard shaft. His toes curled and he moaned. The vibrations sent me spiraling down waves and waves of pleasure. I was wild, but he wouldn't let me go. The faster I went, the faster he went until he suddenly tensed. He tapped me lightly on the ass.

I came off his cock to demand, "Harder." And then I went back to sucking on the tip and tasting the precum with wide swathes of my tongue.

"I'm going to come. I want to be inside you when I do."

"Where are the condoms?" I asked, staggering off him.

"Jeans." He pointed.

Ripping open the three pack, I got one out. My fingers were shaking as I slid it onto his throbbing cock. "You want a lap dance, mister?" I asked, guiding him inside me.

"Yes," he groaned. His hands on my hips were helping me bounce on his hardness. I felt like I could fly. The lights of the Las Vegas Strip gleamed bright neon through the curtains as I rode him. His eyes were closed, but his fingers rubbed me. We were going so fast that he barely touched my clit with each rocking motion, but it was enough. I squeezed down hard on him when I came. Miles slammed my hips down and thrust up one last time. I nearly toppled over like last time, but he held me in place.

We moved slowly then, unwilling to stop. I finally shivered and he gently rolled me off. When he went into the bathroom to clean up, I turned toward the window again and looked out at the Strip. Las Vegas Jackie could have this every night.

Miles slid back into bed and pulled me into his side. "I want you to stay away from the club for the rest of your vacation."

"Why?" I asked sleepily, a little hurt.

"Too dangerous with the gang activity. I don't want you to become a target because you're special to me."

Propping myself up on an elbow, I stared down at him. "I'm special to you?"

He nodded, his eyes already closed.

"You're special to me too," I whispered in his ear and followed him into sleep.

CHAPTER TWENTY

Miles Carvello

I hated wearing the fucking wire. I thought it looked obvious as shit, but Grier assured me it didn't. I also hated giving five thousand dollars to Leonidas, even if everyone else on the block thought it was the cost of doing business.

"I'm going to get my money back, right?"

"It will be evidence, but yeah, after the trial you get it back." Grier did some last minute tests on the microphone. "Try to get him in here if you can. But if you can't, sit as far away from the speakers as possible. Don't put yourself at risk, but try to get him to talk about what he's doing. I want to get him on racketeering, but if we can pin a drug charge on him, I'd like to see what he offers in exchange for immunity."

"I'll do what I can."

I tried to act normal. Grier was waiting in the men's room until we officially opened and then he was going to take a seat up front. He probably was going to hire Miranda for a few lap dances while I made the deal with Leonidas.

Sitting down at my desk, I opened the drawer and took out the album that my uncle had kept about me. Every time I made the papers or was mentioned in a magazine, he had cut it out and put it in here. There were pictures of us too. Me on my first night on the security team. He and I with our arms around the burlesque dancers.

That made me think of Jackie. She was probably still in the air or about to land in Carson City. Her lunch date was going to be about as much fun as mine. I wished I could have gone with her. She had woken up nervous and freaking out about meeting Parker and verbally sparring with Lisa.

I smiled at how I had relaxed her a bit. My cock throbbed as I thought about how hot and wet she'd felt when I fucked her up against the window while she looked out over the Strip. I was looking forward to doing it again tonight. And for the rest of the nights of the next week. I hadn't given up the idea of convincing her to stay, but when she was so wrapped up in knots about Lisa, I didn't want to add to her stress.

While I was checking all the stations and making sure the bar was fully stocked with clean glasses and enough booze, I ran into Paulie in the kitchen. He looked like someone had beaten the shit out of him.

"What happened to you?" I asked.

"I got into a car accident." He turned away from me to unload plates from the dishwasher to the prep station.

I looked closer. "Before or after you took a beating? Don't bullshit me. I know what it looks like when you get worked over."

"I don't want to talk about it."

"Too bad. When you didn't show up for work, guess what I found in your locker?"

He shrugged. "I don't know."

"Don't you? Is that why you got knocked around?"

"I don't know what you're talking about, man."

Liu was trying to get my attention from the walk-in, so I let Paulie off the hook. I hoped Leonidas was a little more talkative. Of course Grier thought Paulie had been set up, so maybe the gun and the baggies had been planted there after Paulie left.

"What?" I said, aggravated, leaning against the big refrigerator door.

"You're not going to believe this shit," he said, handing me a tray of meats and cheese. "That asshole Zeke wants his job back."

That was interesting. "What do you think?"

"He was good when he was here. I don't like that he took off without notice, but we could use people we don't have to train. And you took back Paulie, so why not Zeke?"

"I think Zeke might be running his own business out of the club. Escorts," I said at Liu's look. I wasn't going to tell him about Dee's newest profession because it wasn't his business. But I didn't want Zeke leading away any of the dancers to Pahrump.

"His sister is a good worker," Liu said. "I'd bet she'd keep an eye on him."

"If you want him, he's yours. Don't let him know that I suspect he's up to no good. If he's clean, no problem. If he's messing around, I want to catch him in the act."

"Deal."

A few more rounds with security, the DJ, and of course the girls, and we were ready to open. Some clubs were twenty-four hours, but I closed my doors at four a.m. and opened them back up at noon. I only needed about six hours of sleep a night. I had been doing this every day for two years. I was getting sick of the inside of the club. If Jackie did stay in Las Vegas, maybe I'd ask Highway if he wanted to be promoted to manager and we'd split up the shifts. Maybe I'd do it even if Jackie went home.

I signaled for the DJ to start playing and three dancers sauntered into place on each of the small U-shaped stages.

"Open the doors," I said to the doorman. I was pleased that there had been a small line. At the end of the line were Leonidas and his lieutenants.

"You got the money?" he asked when he got to where I was standing in the middle of the club.

"You've got the information?"

Leonidas nodded.

"You want to do this out here or in my office?"

"We might want some privacy for this conversation."

I shrugged as if it didn't matter and led them back to my office. I saw Grier and Miranda getting up from their usual table. He followed her into the VIP room just as I reached my office. The goons sat on the couch and Leonidas perched a hip on my desk. He glanced at Uncle Johnny's album and I inwardly cursed. I couldn't believe I'd left it out.

"That you as a kid?"

"Me and my uncle." I tossed him the five thousand dollars. It was rolled up and secured with a rubber band.

He lobbed it to one of his lieutenants on the couch to count it.

"You've been waiting a long time for this," he said.

"It better be accurate information."

"It is. You've been staring at them for the last two years." He jerked his thumb behind him. "Konner and Dieter from the pawn shop across the street had it in for your uncle for years. Surely, you remember that?"

"I remember that there was no love lost between them, but murder and arson? I don't buy it. The cops didn't either when they questioned them back then."

"Konner and Dieter are mob connected. They're not big

fish, but they know people who are. While you were hustling drunks and laying socialites in Mykonos, Johnny was struggling financially."

My jaw clenched. I hadn't known it at the time, but after the fire I had been stuck with settling his estate. He had been a few months from bankruptcy when he died.

"Your uncle went to Konner and Dieter and said he wanted to cash in on the club's insurance policy. He hired them to burn it down."

I was shaking my head in denial. But in my gut, it sounded right.

"He was getting old and getting sick of the club. He wasn't bringing in the crowd that he had been in the seventies and eighties. He wanted a lump sum to move to Florida and live the good life. He even had a girl picked out to take with him." Leonidas handed me a photograph. For a second, I expected to see one of the burlesque dancers I knew from the old days. Instead I saw a younger version of Dee's mother. "Her name is Eleanor Brandon. But she went by the stage name Brandy."

"What the fuck?" I said. Brandy hadn't been around while I had been there. And Dee's mom hadn't mentioned that she had known my uncle.

"You can confirm my story with her. Her number is on the back of the picture. Anyway, at the last minute, your uncle got cold feet. Dieter and Konner were annoyed, but they were willing to stop it—as long as they got a cut of the insurance money."

"If there was no fire, there would be no money."

"Exactly. Your uncle didn't have it and he wasn't willing to go on a payment plan. They threatened Brandy. So he decided to take matters in his own hands, or at least that's what Dieter and Konner's story is going to be. Johnny tried to burn his own bar down and got caught in the blaze."

"That didn't happen."

"No, it didn't. Brandy convinced him to let Dieter and Konner go with the original plan. Your uncle reluctantly agreed. Meanwhile, Dieter and Konner made Brandy a better offer than Florida. High-priced escort who could hand select her clients and keep fifty percent. Brandy was no fool. She'd rather have her own money and retire after a few years than be Johnny Dalton's arm candy in Florida. Johnny got so mad that he went after Dieter and Konner. They killed him and left his body in the club."

"Why would Brandy confirm this with me?"

"Because Dieter and Konner recently convinced her daughter to follow in her mother's footsteps and she's pissed. She wants revenge."

That was news to me. I thought it had been Zeke that started Dee on being an escort. I kept my mouth shut because it was possible that Zeke was working with Dieter and Konner. Or they got wind of Dee's new job in Pahrump and decided to make her a nicer offer.

"How do you know all this?" I asked Leonidas, who was looking very pleased with himself.

"It's my business to know what happens in my territory. It's a business that would be very lucrative to you. I could keep tabs on all your staff. I knew all of this before you even had a clue. You had a line cook who decided to become a prostitute." Leonidas counted off on his fingers. "Then there's your dishwasher who couldn't pay his loan shark on time, so he tried to run, but got caught and punished with a very generous warning." He leaned in toward me. "I'd start looking for another dishwasher soon. If he misses another payment . . ." Leonidas drew a finger across his throat. "Let's see, what else? Oh, yes, your dancers. You fired one who was supplementing her income, but then you asked her to come back. Does your girlfriend know about that? Speaking of the lovely La Vie Bohème, did you know she went straight from your bed this morning and got on a plane to Carson City? She's looking for a burlesque job. You should have let her keep dancing in the club."

I forced my fists to unclench when he mentioned Jackie. He was wrong about the second part so that meant all he knew was where she was and that she had auditioned somewhere. But he didn't know it had been at the Odyssey casino. I was glad for his overconfidence, but I hated that Jackie was on this douchebag's radar. I decided to play him a bit and see what else I could find out from. "That would be a valuable service, but aren't Konner and Dieter your clients? Are you going to roll over on me to an interested party one day?"

"That depends on you. Konner and Dieter are chafing at the money I charge because you're not paying me. They threatened to get some of their mob boys to muscle me and mine around like you did a few years ago. You're bad for business, Miles. I'm hoping by this show of faith, I can convince you that it's safer all around to pay me ten grand a month."

"I told you, I can't be profitable and pay you."

"We could work something out," he said. "Ginny is very eager to be a major part of your business and mine."

"Ginny is a fine dancer."

"And a good salesgirl too."

"What are you saying?" I needed him to spell it out.

"I'm saying either you let Ginny sell my drugs out of your club or I'm going to kidnap your girl and send her down to a group of friends of mine in Egypt, who'd pay nicely for a blond stripper slave girl. You'll never see La Vie Bohème again. Do we have an understanding?"

I slammed his face into my desk as soon as he finished speaking, putting all my weight into making sure that smarmy smile hit solid oak with extreme prejudice. "Red alert," I said into my Bluetooth as I banged his head a few more times, making sure that his nose was spaghetti.

The goons tried to come at me, but I was behind the desk and their boss's body was stretched across it. I was pretty sure Leonidas was unconscious and missing a few teeth. "Put those knives down or you're going to be using them as suppositories," I snarled.

My security team rushed in with nine millimeters. Highway was going to be pissed he'd missed all the action. "Call the cops," I said. "These pieces of shit attacked me."

"That's bullshit," one of the goons said.

"Tell it to the judge."

———

Jackie Mitchell

This had to be the world's most awkward chicken salad sandwich. Half of it nearly landed in my lap after my sister informed me she was now vegan. Parker was easily twice her age. He was a good-looking man with silver hair. Lisa had gushed to me in the bathroom that he was her silver fox. He seemed like a decent enough guy, though. The age difference gave me pause, but I was trying to keep an open mind.

"Have you ever thought of being a private detective?" Parker joked. Lisa linked her fingers through his and laughed.

She looked happier than I'd ever seen her.

"No, I don't have the patience. Look, Parker, I'm sure Lisa has told you about our mother."

"In detail."

"It's all true," I said. "Just in case you think she was exaggerating. But that being said, she *is* a mother and she's very worried about her youngest daughter. Do you have children?"

"I have fraternal twins. They just started UCLA this year. My ex lives out in California, so they were able to get in-state tuition. It helped a great deal, but college is very expensive."

"Is that why you asked Lisa to help you get funding for the show?"

"You don't have to answer that," Lisa said, squeezing his hand tighter. "I told her it was none of her business."

"She's your sister and she's worried I'm taking advantage of you. Would you rather explain it to her or to your mother?"

Lisa grimaced.

"I'm not accusing you of anything," I said. "I just want to understand. Lisa was in a bad way after her surgery. When she left for Las Vegas, I was glad she was getting a change of scene. But then she stopped answering phone calls and we got increasingly worried."

"And your mother sent you down here to save her from herself."

"Yeah," I admitted.

"Like you've done so many times before."

"Not that many," Lisa said mulishly.

"What would ease your mind?" Parker asked.

I was trying to figure out how to phrase my questions. They all sounded like I was prying into Lisa's personal affairs and none of what I wanted to know was any of my business.

"Just spit it out." Lisa rolled her eyes.

"How much is Lisa's salary?"

"She doesn't get one. She gets a percentage of the house," Parker said calmly.

I winced. "What percentage?"

"Fifty-fifty because she is also the coproducer."

"Is that in writing?" I asked Lisa.

"Yes," she groaned at me.

"May I see the contract?"

"No."

"Darling, what harm could that do?" Parker said, kissing the back of her hand.

"I don't know where my copy is," she admitted.

Before I could go nuclear, Parker said, "I can e-mail it to you later today. My attorneys drew it up so that it was a fair contract."

I was leaning toward believing him. "If everything is on the up-and-up, all you need to do is call Mom and tell her you're producing your own show in Carson City. She'll be thrilled. After that, just answer her calls once in a while and everything will be back to normal."

Lisa snorted. "I don't want to call her until the show is successful. I don't want her to build it up in her mind just to have me fail again."

Now it was my turn to snort. "When have you ever failed? You're the golden child."

"Yeah, I'm so golden that if I don't talk to my mother once a week, she thinks I've hurt myself or been led astray by con artists. Unlike you. She trusts you with everything."

I blinked at her in shock before staring back down at my chicken salad. There were walnuts and cut up red grapes in it. I couldn't decide if it was delicious or weird. Why not both? That was easier to think about than the fact that Lisa seemed to be resentful of my relationship with our mother.

"Why didn't you want me to come to opening night?" That had been bothering me all last night—well the noncheesecake and Miles portion of the night.

"I was afraid I was going to bomb. I was a terrible exotic dancer. I watched the prostitutes at the brothel for tips about being sexy and I couldn't figure that out either. My leg can't support me like it used to. I created a routine where I didn't have to put stress on my knee. I didn't know if it would work or if I'd make a fool out of myself."

"I told her it was brilliant, but she didn't believe me," Parker said.

"You wouldn't like it, Jackie," Lisa said. "It's sexy, flirty and a little dirty." She blushed.

"Chance liked it," I said. He had texted me this morning. The bachelor party was already back in Vegas. We were going to meet at Dalton's later.

"How did you meet Chance Bateman?" Lisa leaned in eagerly.

"He paid me a hundred dollars to give him a lap dance." I went back to my chicken salad and enjoyed Lisa's expression. "But that was just one night. I'm dating Miles Carvello."

"Miles?" Lisa said with a numb expression.

"He's the owner of Dalton's," I explained to Parker, who was looking between us in confusion.

"When did you two meet?" Lisa's confusion was the perfect payback.

"Monday." Had it only been one week?

"You started dating him this week?" she screeched.

"And I auditioned for a stage show at the Odyssey casino. I went on my second callback yesterday. That's why I wasn't here on opening night, not that you invited me. Chance was doing me a favor by taking my place and coming to talk to you."

"Who *are* you?" Lisa gawked at me.

"I'm Las Vegas Jackie." I reached across the table. "Nice to meet you."

CHAPTER TWENTY-ONE

Miles Carvello

Grier was pissed off at me. I suppose I could have handled it better.

"If he wants to file assault charges on you, you're guilty as hell."

I shrugged. "Let him. His rep will be in tatters for being a little snitch bitch who can't take a punch."

"That was more than a punch. You broke a few bones."

"You heard what he said. And now you've got a line on a sex trafficking setup."

"I'm working on it."

We were sharing a bottle of Johnny Walker blue label in my office. My feet were on my desk and I raised my glass. "To Uncle Johnny."

Grier, on the couch, saluted me with his glass. "Don't you make a fucking move on Dieter and Konner next door. Those assholes are all mine."

"When are you going to pick them up?"

"I'm going to pay a visit to that Brandy woman and get a statement. They'll get taken in for questioning as soon as I can push the paperwork through."

"Then what are you still doing here?"

"I need to let you know that Leonidas is going to retaliate once he's out on bond."

"How long is that going to take?" I asked.

"I'd be surprised if he's not out by dinnertime. He knows where your girlfriend is. You need to warn her and don't let her come back to Dalton's until we can lock down the Rivs. Leonidas is going to be out for your blood. I'll put a tail on him, but he's a slippery bastard. We're trying to get a few warrants out on him to stall the process, but he's lawyered up well. It's going to be an uphill battle."

"Damn it," I said, slamming my glass on the table.

"Just a few more weeks."

"I don't have a few more weeks. I suppose you need me to stay local."

"I'd appreciate it."

I wanted to bang my own head on my desk.

Grier tossed back the rest of his drink and stood up. "Thanks for everything. I'll give you the all clear when we nail this asshole, but in the meantime watch your back."

After Grier left, I called Jackie.

"Hi," she said, her voice happy and breathless. My gut unclenched. She was all right. "I'm going to stay over in Carson City another night. I want to see Lisa's show."

"Good. How did everything go?"

"Not as bad as I feared, but not as well as I'd hoped."

"That's the way it goes sometimes," I said, wondering again how I was going to convince her to stay in Carson City.

"I'm going to crash on Parker and Lisa's couch tonight, but I'll be back on the first flight out tomorrow."

"Yeah, about that, I've got some good news and bad news."

"What's going on? You sound weird."

"The police may have found my uncle's murderers."

"That's great! Why don't you sound happy about that?"

"It's going to take a while to build the case, but remember the local gang I was telling you about?"

"The Rivs?"

"Yeah, they're extorting me for money, and they said if I don't pay up they're going to kidnap you and traffic you to someone who wants a blond sex slave."

"What?!"

"They knew you were in Carson City and they knew you were looking at the burlesque show. I'm going to need you to stay close to Lisa and Parker."

"I can't do that after tonight. I'm already on tenuous ground. Having me for a houseguest for another week might destroy the peace Lisa and I have tentatively agreed to. Why can't I just hang out at the Wynn and you can come visit me?"

"I'd love that. Truly. I don't want to say goodbye so soon, but I believe the threat. I think maybe you should cut your vacation short and go back to New York. Save the week of vacation and come back down when the coast is clear." I couldn't believe I was saying this.

"When's that going to be?"

"I don't know. Hopefully not long, but it's not going to happen in a few days. Leonidas has people in Pahrump and Carson City, as well as Las Vegas. I don't want you in their sights."

"I wanted to say goodbye to Chance in person. And I never thought that last night would be the last time we saw each other."

"It's not forever. I'm not ready to end this, are you?"

"No," she said shakily. "I've never done a long-distance relationship before. Is that what you want?"

"Yes," I said firmly.

"Are we exclusive?"

"Yes."

"That's going to take a lot of trust," she said.

"On both our ends. Are you willing to try?"

"Yeah," she said, but she sounded so heartbroken I wanted to do anything I could to make it up to her. Grier had told me to stay put, but in Carson City I'd only be about an hour flight away. It was just for one night.

"Look, why don't you get a hotel room at the airport? Once I make sure everything is settled here tonight, I'll fly in and we can have one more night together."

"You don't have to do that," Jackie said.

"I want to." This was going to be a lean month, with all the money I was throwing around, but I didn't care. I needed one more night to get me through the long months ahead.

"All right," she said, perking up. "I'll call you with the room number."

After she hung up, I had another glass of the scotch and wondered if that had been the right thing to do. The club needed me to be here. How the crap was I going to explain all of this to Highway and still justify leaving tonight? I knew I had to start trusting my people to do their jobs without me watching over them because I was burning out fast.

"It's one night," I said to Johnny Walker. The bottle didn't answer me back.

"Boss, a couple of cops want to talk to you," Mav said into my Bluetooth.

Now what?

"Be right there."

Two of Las Vegas's finest were standing at the door. It wasn't a good sign that they weren't watching the girls. They were watching me, and their hands were on the butts of their pistols. I spread my hands out to my sides to show them I wasn't carrying anything.

"What can I do for you?" I asked.

"Miles Carvello, you're under arrest for the attempted murder of Leonidas Kiryakis."

"If I wanted that shitbag dead, I wouldn't have stopped hitting his head on my desk."

One of the cops winced and said, "Sir, you have the right to remain silent. I suggest you shut the hell up."

I listened to the rest of the Miranda rights and let them cuff me. "Call Highway and get me bonded out," I said to Mav as they led me into the police car.

CHAPTER TWENTY-TWO

Jackie Mitchell

It was the Mondayest of all Mondays.

Miles had ghosted me.

I wouldn't have believed it was possible after our last conversation. He never showed up at the hotel Saturday night and he hadn't returned any of my phone calls. After what he saw me go through with Lisa, Miles should have known how much that type of blow-off would hurt me.

I called Dalton's that night and spoke to someone. They said Miles was busy and that he'd call me back. Yeah, I was busy too. Busy kicking myself for letting a vacation fling get serious. I had to remember it like I did my twenty-first birthday party. We had a great time. We had great sex. And now it was over and that was okay.

New York in January really sucked. It was even worse when we were expecting another snowstorm and my body was wishing I was back in the desert. But instead of lounging on a rooftop bar after being thoroughly sexed, I was at my desk at the Zimmerman Agency. After my long flight, I passed out and slept straight through until my alarm woke me up. There was no way I was going to spend the day moping around my apartment all alone. I took a quick shower and grabbed a bagel from a street vendor as my breakfast. It was damn cold, but at least the food was good.

My mother called almost before I'd finished my first cup of coffee. At least she had waited that long. "Did you find her?" was the first thing out of her mouth.

"Yes. She's alive and well and producing a show in Carson City."

"Producing?" my mother squealed. "What type of show?"

"It's a vaudeville dance show," I hedged. That was close enough. "She's been utterly swamped these past few weeks trying to get backers and with the day-to-day management of putting together the event. That's why she hasn't had time to return our calls." I hated covering for Lisa. But I knew this was what my mother wanted to hear. "I wasn't there for opening night, but I was able to see the show. It was wonderful."

And it was. I had been proud of Lisa. We had underestimated her. She'd found a way to dance without hurting her knee. She'd found a boyfriend who was kind and supportive. I rubbed the stabbing pain in the center of my chest. I told myself it was heartburn from drinking my coffee.

"I completely understand. It all makes sense."

"I took pictures. I'll send them over later." They were highly edited and showed Lisa in front of the theater, strategically covering the poster.

My mother let out a long sigh. "I'm so glad she's a producer."

"You're welcome," I said. "I'll send over my expenses for reimbursement later once I get settled. I'm in the office today."

"You're back in New York?"

"No reason to stay," I said, trying not to sound like Eeyore.

"Just give me the bottom line. No sense in going through all that paperwork."

My eyebrows raised. She was in a good mood. I decided to elaborate to head off any uncomfortable questions. "Lisa's living in Carson City, Nevada in order to be closer to where the theater is."

"I can't wait to talk to her."

"She might not be able to call back. Remember, she's still recovering from her surgeries." That was a total lie, but it was one my mother would accept, and it would buy Lisa some time to figure out when and how much she was going to tell Mom. "She's burning the candle at both ends. She spends all her free time sleeping when she's not working on the show."

Another call was coming through. It was a Las Vegas number.

"Mom, I've got to take another call."

"Wait," she said. "I want to hear all about the show."

"I can't right now. I'm working. I'll call you later." After all, *I* didn't have a show to do. All I had waiting for me at home was a pint of Ben and Jerry's ice cream, which I would have for dessert after I scarfed down some pizza. I had missed the taste of New York pizza.

By the time I switched over, the call went to voice mail. It hadn't been Miles's number or Chance's. Whoever it was, was leaving a long message. It was hellishly early in Las Vegas, but I dialed Chance's number anyway hoping he knew what was going on.

"Are you okay, luv?" he asked, sounding like he had just risen from the dead.

"I'm so sorry for calling so early." He must have known Miles had dumped me. "I'm doing all right. I'm a little sad and everything seems so bleak, but I'll manage. I just wanted to call and let you know that everything went really well with me and Lisa. I'm sorry I couldn't say goodbye in person."

"Why is that? Dalton's may be gone, but we can meet up at the Drag Queen Diner. Bring Miles. I've got a proposition for him."

"What do you mean Dalton's is gone?" I sat up straight in my chair.

"The fire. It's completely gutted."

"Fire?" I shrieked.

A few people poked their heads into my office, but I waved them frantically away.

"Shit, I thought you knew. Aren't you with Miles?"

"Chance, I'm in New York. I haven't spoken to Miles since Saturday morning. Is he all right? Was he inside the bar when it caught on fire?" I held my hand on my stomach, trying not to throw up. Miles had warned me that it was dangerous for me to be in the club, but I never thought that it was also dangerous for him.

"Get this. He was in jail at the time."

"Jail?"

"He assaulted a gang leader and the gang leader pressed charges. Miles couldn't get a bail bondsman because they're all in the gang's back pocket. Highway managed to haul someone out of bed on Sunday to bail Miles out, but by then it was too late. There's nothing but slag and wreckage."

"Was anyone hurt?"

"I don't think so. I haven't spoken to him. I only got the skinny because I saw Mav at Caesar's last night."

"That fire was set." I banged my fist on the desk. "It was arson."

"I think so too."

"Where's Miles?" I asked.

"I don't know. I thought he was with you. He was going to go out to Carson City last I heard."

"I'm not there," I said in a small voice. Why didn't he call? Did he lose his phone in the fire?

"Fuck a duck. I'll see what I can find out."

"I'll see too." I bundled back into my coat and my boots, cursing myself. I should have known that Miles would never ghost me. He was the only person in my life who had ever put me first. I had to go back and find him.

"Where the hell are you going?" my boss said.

"Back to Vegas."

"No, you're not. You just got back this morning."

"I had an emergency come up."

She groaned. "Not Lisa again."

"I'll explain later."

"You're lucky you still have some vacation time left. You better hurry or you're going to get stranded on the tarmac. There's a storm coming in."

I ran outside and hailed a cab. It was a good thing I hadn't unpacked yet.

CHAPTER TWENTY-THREE

Miles Carvello

The worst part of all of this was the memories. The smell of burned wires and broken dreams. I walked through the wreckage. It had been arson all right. Mav had smelled the gasoline when he was doing his final rounds at four a.m. He had tried to put it out with a fire extinguisher, but it had spread too fast. At least he had enough time to clear the building and no one got hurt.

"Miles?"

I had to do a double take. I almost didn't recognize Ginny in street clothes and sneakers. "Not now," I said. I didn't have the energy to fight. I was still sporting a hangover from drinking myself to sleep on Highway's couch last night.

She walked up to me anyway, steadying herself as she climbed over the rubble. "This is for you." She pressed a compact disk in my hands.

"What's this?"

"This is the security footage from the bail bondsman office. You didn't get it from me."

Both Konner and Dieter's pawn shop and the bail bondsman had claimed their security cameras had been off last night. Our tapes burned up in the fire. There had been no evidence except for circumstantial, just like when my uncle's club was torched.

"How did you get it?"

"I took it from Leonidas, who took it from the bondsman."

"He's going to kill you. We have to get you protection."

"Look, I'm not stupid," Ginny said. "No matter what you think. He's not going to realize it's missing. I swapped it with one of Dee's CDs. He destroyed the evidence this morning." She put finger quotes around the word "evidence."

"Dee?"

"Yeah, she told me keep away from Dalton's Saturday night, so I stayed at her apartment in Pahrump. Leonidas came by with a few friends after he got bailed out." She gave a chuckle. "You did a number on his face. He was already bragging that Dalton's was going to burn to the ground. He got Zeke to do it."

"Zeke?"

"Yeah, Zeke's been trying to patch into the Rivs forever. He thought having Dee be an escort for them would get him in. But then she decided she liked working at a brothel instead. Don't get me wrong, she still freelances—which is why Leonidas came by last night. Zeke would have done anything Leonidas said to become a full member of the Rivs. I watched the footage. You can see Zeke coming in with the gas cans in the confusion when the cops took you away. And it shows him torching your car as he left the building after closing time.

"That son of a bitch," I said.

Movement caught my eye and I saw Grier shambling down the sidewalk toward us. He was in his homeless person disguise. No one even blinked at him.

"Why are you telling me this? I thought you and Leonidas had a deal."

"We did. I sold his drugs and he'd leave my baby sister alone."

"Did you tell him about Jackie?"

Ginny looked away. "Yeah. I didn't think he'd go psycho."

"Are you willing to tell the police what you know? It's the only way to keep him away from your sister for good."

She shook her head. "He'll come after her if I take the witness stand. You don't need me. You've got the evidence. Zeke will turn over on Leonidas."

"Not if he wants to be a loyal gang member," I said. "He'll go to jail first."

"Oh, Miles." Ginny reached up and rubbed my cheek affectionately. "Not everyone is like you. There's a reason Zeke has been only a pledge of the Rivs for most of his life. He's a weasel." She stood up on her tiptoes and tried to kiss me on the lips. I turned my head just in time and she got my cheek. "We could have been good together. You would have protected my sister."

"You should have come to me."

"You should have come to *me*, but you were never interested. I hope Jackie appreciates what she's got." With a sigh, Ginny walked away.

Jackie was safe in New York and that was all that mattered. That's what her sister Lisa had said when I hauled ass to Carson City yesterday. I was caught between being relieved and being gutted. She was the one person I needed to speak to. If I couldn't hold her in my arms, I just wanted to hear her voice.

I would have called her, but my phone was dead, and the

cord was ash under my feet. It was on my list to get another one, but I had to figure out where the hell I was going to live in the meantime.

Grier came up to me next. "I'm sorry about the club and for the bullshit arrest Saturday night. We're looking into why you couldn't get bonded out right away. I'm not the type of guy that says, 'Heads will roll,' but it's someone's ass, that's for damn sure. All I can say is Leonidas didn't torch your place. He was in Pahrump."

I was pissed, but I knew there was only so much Grier could have done. Shielding my actions from the security cameras that were still operational on this street, I passed him the CD. "Dalton's missing security tape. My waiter Zeke did it on Leonidas's orders."

I told him what Ginny had told me and he sped away to act on the new information. Hopefully, he'd get a warrant out on both Leonidas and Zeke. With my wire conversation and this new evidence, I had a feeling that the Rivs were going to lose a lot of power.

"You've got nothing to worry about. The assault charges against you will be dropped and Leonidas and his boys won't be around to bother you once the district attorney gets ahold of them."

I hadn't been concerned about the assault charges. I had a good lawyer. As for Leonidas and the Rivs, well I guess that depended on how good their lawyer was.

"Go get 'em," I said and turned away to look at the ruins of my bar again. When Grier had left the area, I closed my eyes. "I did it," I said, wondering if Uncle Johnny was listening.

Sitting down on a pile of rubble, I poked through the twisted metal hoping to find something that had survived. I wasn't sure how long I sat there, but it was getting dark. I needed to get my head out of my ass and get a hotel room for the night. My back popped as I stretched. A car skidded to a stop and I immediately tensed for a fight. If they had a gun, I was toast, but if they only had knives, I was looking forward to getting out some aggression.

"Miles," Jackie said, coming around the car and running over to me.

I met her halfway and hauled her up and out of the wreckage. "Are you out of your mind? I told you it wasn't safe here. Get in the car."

Once we were driving away from Dalton's, I didn't know whether to yell at her or kiss her.

"Don't you yell at me about safe," she said. "You didn't tell me that you were a target too."

"Arrogance," I said. Grabbing her hand, I put it up to my mouth. "I'm glad you didn't go home."

"Actually, I did. And then Chance told me what happened, and I came back."

"Your jet lag must have jet lag," I said.

"I'm running on energy drinks and sugar. We're going to have our week together, even if we have to leave the state to do it."

"I think I can find the time." I leaned my head back on the headrest, content to let her drive us wherever she wanted to go. I didn't care as long as I was with her.

"Oh, Miles, your poor club."

Yeah, I was sorry to see it go too. "If it brings Uncle Johnny's murderers to justice, it will all have been worth it. I have no idea what the hell I'm going to do now. I'm a little old to be jetting all over Europe to beat people up."

"You don't have to think about that now," she said. "We're together and that's all that matters."

It was a small bright spot that she and I seemed to be on the same page about that. "Jackie, I know we've only known each other a week and my life is a complete shitstorm right now, but I'm falling for you."

She gave a watery chuckle. "That's good because I'm head over heels for you too."

"I don't suppose you still have your reservation at the Wynn?"

"As a matter of fact, I do. I wanted to make sure I'd be able to pay someone to go to my room and pack my things I left behind and mail them to New York for me."

"I could use a shower and to spend the rest of the night making love to you."

"That's the best offer I've had all day." At the next stoplight, she leaned over and kissed me. "However, we have to make a stop first. Have you eaten yet?"

Now that she mentioned it, I was starving and not just for her delicious body. "I could eat."

"Do you like drag queens?

———

Jackie Mitchell

Chance was serenading Marilyn Monroe with his rendition of "Don't Be Cruel" when we walked in. He saw us and did a final Elvis hip pivot for the crowd and waved us over to a booth.

"Miles, how are you holding up?" They did the dude bro hug and we sat down.

"I'm not sure." Miles slung his arm over me, and I cuddled into him. "But I'm better because she's here."

"I can see that."

The waitress came and we ordered a mountain of food. I made sure to order a pot of coffee. "And keep it coming."

There was no way in hell I was falling asleep before I got the full Miles Carvello treatment in my nice big bed in the Wynn.

"Where's the rest of the blokes?" Miles asked.

"They've gone back home to 'Straya," he said. "I'm heading back to California. My sister Adele and my Mom need me."

"Is there anything I can do?" I asked.

"Nah, it's a family thing. You know how it is."

I did. "If you ever need anything, call me."

"I've got your number. I'm not going to lose it. Besides, I think me and your man here might be doing some business."

Miles looked up from his coffee. "Are you looking to hire a bouncer? I've got impeccable references."

"I'm looking to invest in some Las Vegas property."

Miles put his cup down.

"I really liked Lisa's show. Don't get me wrong. I love strippers."

Strip-pahs.

I loved his accent.

"But the burlesque seemed so classy. It was sexy, sensual, and alluring. I think a club like that would make a killing where Dalton's used to be."

"You want me to rebuild. Again."

"And this time, you're not going to do it all by yourself," I butted in. "You're going to have Highway and the rest of the Dalton's crew to help out. And me."

"You're going to help all the way from New York?" Miles asked.

"No. I'm moving to Las Vegas. I figure even if I don't get a job being a showgirl, I can always try my hand at being an agent down here. And it's not like I'm going to stop audition-ing." I'd get a part eventually and I would do it while helping Miles. I bit my lip. "That is, if you don't think I'd get in the way."

"I have nothing to offer you. I'm homeless."

"We'll figure it out," I said.

"I'm loaded," Chance said. "Or at least well off enough to front you some money. We can do a fifty-fifty split. And if the place is successful, we can open one up in California. Or if you don't want to be partners, you can buy me out."

"This feels like charity," Miles said, scowling into his coffee.

"It's capitalism, you lunkhead."

Miles smirked. "Are you going to get up on stage and do a routine?"

"I might. I might even make that a term of our agreement."

"I need a picture of this auspicious occasion." Sliding out of my seat, I stepped back to get a shot of them.

"Now you two," Chance said, grabbing my phone.

I wrapped my arms around Miles's chest and let all my happiness show. New York Jackie was no more. Make way for Las Vegas Jackie.

"You got a voice mail message, luv." Chance handed me back my phone.

"I hope it's not your mother," Miles groaned.

"Oh, it's that call from this morning." I had completely forgotten about it. "Excuse me while I check it."

Miles and Chance lowered their voices and started to hammer out the details as I dialed into my voice mail.

"Hi, this message is for Jackie Mitchell. This is Simi Pierce from the Odyssey casino. We were very impressed with your audition and we'd like to offer you a position in our show Travesty. *Please call me at your earliest convenience."*

I clamped my hand on Miles's arm and squeezed tight. He broke off what he was saying. "Jackie, what's wrong?"

"I got the job. I'm going to dance in *Travesty* at the Odyssey,"

EPILOGUE – ONE YEAR LATER

I was going to puke. "Lisa, where the fuck are my fans?"

"Behind the sofa where you left them."

Lisa was in red and I was in black. We were dressed like flappers from the roaring twenties. I had a night off from *Travesty* and my sister and I were going to do the first number at Miles and Chance's newly opened club, Uncle Johnny's Burlesque Show. With Chance's money and Miles' connections, rebuilding had been a breeze. Of course, not having the pressure of the Rivs or any other gang activity might have helped as well. Shortly after I moved in with Miles, Leonidas had been killed while out on bail. And after a few more strategic arrests, the Rivs faded into Las Vegas history like the casino they had named themselves after.

"I can't believe Mom isn't backstage nagging us," Lisa said.

"I told Highway and Mav that it was their asses if she got past them."

Lisa and I had practiced this act for over a month in our spare time. She had choreographed it, and it was amazing. Because our father was also in the audience, Lisa and I wouldn't be doing anything erotic. We were going to do a fan dance to some swinging jazz to warm up the crowd. Then there would be a comedian and more dancing. The good stuff didn't happen until after midnight and I was hoping my parents would go back to the hotel long before that.

"How are we doing, ladies?" Parker said, coming into the dressing room. He gave Lisa a kiss on the cheek and smiled at me. "You both look beautiful."

Lisa dragged him into a private corner to canoodle a bit and I gave them some privacy. Leaving my fans behind, I walked out into the club where the band was playing something slow and hypnotic. My parents were on the dance floor. I waved at my father and he gave me a thumbs-up.

"Hey gorgeous." Miles pulled me in for a kiss. "Nervous?"

"No. You?"

"It's all good."

"I just wish Chance were here to celebrate. It's not fair," I said.

"I know." Miles hugged me. "He'd be here if he could. He said to tell you congratulations."

"For what? Not killing Lisa?"

"I told him that congratulations might be premature, but he didn't think so." Miles handed me a small velvet box.

"What's this? Something to go with my flapper costume?"

"If you want."

I opened it, expecting earrings. Or a hairclip. I hadn't been expecting a diamond ring.

"It's . . . it's . . ."

"Jacqueline Aida Mitchell, I love you. Would you do me the honor of being my wife?"

Miles slipped the marquis-cut diamond on my finger. It flashed in the soft light of the club and with the sequins of my dress. "Yes. Oh, Miles. Yes."

"Don't cry. You'll look like a raccoon."

I threw my arms around his neck. "I love you."

"You're going to knock them dead tonight. Everyone is going to see you for the star that you are."

"How long until the show starts?" I asked, threading my fingers through his and leading him back to his office.

"Long enough," he said, huskily and locked the door behind him.

COCKY HERO CLUB

Want to keep up with all of the new releases in Vi Keeland and Penelope Ward's Cocky Hero Club world? Make sure you sign up for the official Cocky Hero Club newsletter for all the latest on our upcoming books:

https://www.subscribepage.com/CockyHeroClub

Check out other books in the Cocky Hero Club series:

http://www.cockyheroclub.com

MORE BOOKS BY JAMIE K. SCHMIDT

If you liked this book, you may want to try:

Three Sisters Ranch Series
(high heat contemporary romance)

The Cowboy's Daughter

The Cowboy's Hunt

The Cowboy's Heart

Club Inferno Series
(erotic contemporary romance)

USA Today Best Seller: Heat

Longing

Fever

The Emerging Queens Series
(high heat paranormal romance)

The Queen's Mystery – FREE on most e-book retailers!

The Queen's Wings

The Queen's Flight

The Queen's Dance

The Truth & Lies Series
(erotic New Adult romance)

Truth Kills

Truth Reveals

The Hawaii Heat series
(high heat contemporary romance)

USA Today Best Seller: Life's a Beach

Beach Happens

Beach My Life

Beauty and the Beach

The Sentinels of Babylon series
(high heat contemporary romance)

Necessary Evil

Sentinel's Kiss

Warden's Woman (coming soon...)

Ryder's Dream (coming soon...)

Stand-alone novels
(high heat contemporary romance)

2018 Rita® Finalist in Erotic Romance: Stud

Hard Cover

Maiden Voyage

Spice - Book Three in the Fate Series - Co-written with Jenna
Jameson

Wild Wedding Hookup

Holiday Hookup

Stand-alone novels & novellas

Trinity (erotic ménage paranormal romance)

Midnight Lady, (high heat fantasy romance)

Naked Truth (romantic suspense)

Santa Genie (erotic paranormal romance)

Samurai's Heart (erotic paranormal romance)

Betrayed (erotic fantasy romance)

The Handy Men (erotic ménage romance)

Shifter's Price (erotic ménage dystopian paranormal romance)

The Seeker (paranormal romance)

A Spark of Romance (sweet small town romance)

Newsletter Subscriber's First Peek

A Casual Christmas (contemporary romance) – Exclusive to newsletter subscribers for 2017. Now available everywhere.

A Not So Casual Christmas (contemporary romance) – Exclusive to newsletter subscribers for 2018. Now available everywhere.

A Chaotic Christmas (contemporary romance) – Exclusive to newsletter subscribers for 2019. Now available everywhere.

Sign up here to receive the 2020 short story FREE on Christmas eve.

Anthologies & Collections

Graveyard Shift (High heat paranormal romance)

Flash Magic (No heat at all speculative fiction stories)

Manufactured by Amazon.ca
Bolton, ON

28067433R00131